MORE PRAISE FOR *MARLOWE'S REVENGE*

"In *Marlowe's Revenge*, Dan Stuart provides us multilayered characters who walk familiar and coveted sites in their search for reckoning with the city's past, and their own. Their interwoven worlds and lives are both thrilling and fascinating."

—Lydia R. Otero, author of *La Calle: Spatial Conflicts and Urban Renewal in a Southwest City* and *In the Shadows of the Freeway, Growing Up Brown & Queer*

"Finally, Tucson gets the neo-noir novel it deserves: gritty, romantic, broken-hearted, and surprisingly funny."

—Stacey Richter, award-winning author of short story collections *My Date with Satan* and *Twin Study*

"*Marlowe's Revenge* is top rate screwball noir, a finger clicking mix of guns, drugs, golf, and rock & roll. Think Carl Hiassen, Dave Barry, and Laurence Shames, with a little Charles Willeford on the side. Hip, hardboiled, and hilarious."

—Allan Jones, author and former editor of *Melody Maker* and *UNCUT Magazine*

"A merciless, funny and reluctantly empathetic novel that places Dan Stuart's dusty lower Arizona on some fractured literary roadmap between Jim Thompson's West Texas to James Ellroy's Los Angeles. Plus, golf. And a sinking rock & roll star."

—Brian Jabas Smith, author of novel-in-stories *Spent Saints* and *Tucson Salvage: Tales and Recollections from La Frontera*

MARLOWE'S REVENGE

MARLOWE'S REVENGE

DAN STUART

R&R Press, LLC | Tucson, Arizona

R&R Press, LLC
www.r-rpress.com

© 2022 by R&R Press, LLC
All rights reserved. Published 2022

ISBN: 979-8-9857318-0-4 (paperback)

Cover design by Lilly Sara Thaxton
Cover illustration by Rock "Cyfi" Martinez
Interior design and typesetting by Lilly Sara Thaxton

Library of Congress Control Number: 2022932490

Printed in the United States of America
♾ This paper meets the requirements of ANSI/NISO Z39.48-1992 (Permanence of Paper).

For my dad, wish we could play just one more round

INTRODUCTION

I n 1991, I was thirty years old and living in Madrid with my beautiful but duplicitous Spanish wife. I had become addicted to *codeine con lasa* (available over-the-counter for three dollars per bottle) when the company spitefully changed the formula, making it no longer a suitable daily fix. Heroin was plentiful, but much more expensive than the codeine, and my habit soon went up to 5,000 *pesetas* a day. This required frequent trips to Plaza Bilbao to score from a dangerously reliable *gitano*, putting tremendous strain on my marriage. One night in desperation, I called my older sister in Tucson and begged for help. She soon got together with my family, and arranged for me to detox in a fairly reputable recovery center that advertised on late-night TV. A week later, I found myself at Barajas airport, and somehow got on a half-empty 747 to fly home. Using a tin foil cover from the rubber chicken entree, I smoked crude Afghan dope in the bathroom, all the way to Houston, where I had to pass through customs before my connecting flight. Waiting for my luggage, a drug-sniffing beagle made a beeline and promptly sat down beside me. I told his handler that I had indeed been getting high for the last eight hours, but had none left and was on the way to rehab. Maybe it was the end of his shift, or simple kindness, but the officer just shook his head, gave the dog a treat, and wished me luck. So began my most hellish year, 12 months that marked me forever, that I still dream about, that I can't forget. Like the others, this book is 65 percent true, but what is and what isn't gets harder for me to discern with each passing day. Looking back, I hardly recognize myself at all, but feel I must try in order to set things right, perhaps preventing my mind from completely unraveling like it did a decade ago before Oaxaca saved me. Sitting here now in an air-conditioned and hard-plumbed '72 Winnebago, just a few blocks from El Tiradito shrine, it helps that it's 105 degrees outside during a raging pandemic, and I have nothing better to do until I get my hips replaced, so time is not an issue. I might add that Arizona has no statute of limitations for murder, but for most other felonies it's seven years, just in case you were wondering.

Dan Stuart, Tucson, AZ, August 2020

Front Nine

CHAPTER 1

First one out as the sun rose, with only an ancient foursome behind, Marlowe felt like an Apache scout blazing a trail. He'd been clean only a few weeks, but with every round his game was getting better. Playing almost every day, his latest and final publishing advance covered the green fees, still less than half of what he'd been spending on heroin back in Spain. The goal was to get under a 5-handicap; scratch was impossible for a popcorn hitter like him. Golf was a good substitute for dope: ritualistic, decent exercise, and left him with a post-round feeling of calm that allowed for a few precious hours of sleep at night.

Making the turn at Fred Enke, a difficult desert course, Marlowe's drive drifted into the right hardpan after an unlucky bounce off a sprinkler head. Finding his ball beside a jumping cholla, he squinted down to make sure it was indeed a Titleist 3 he always marked with a small M in red ink. Trying to pick it clean, he caught it thin but got some roll, leaving maybe 130 yards to a back right pin. Wary of coming up short, he clubbed down to an 8, but hit it sweet and flew the green into a back bunker he couldn't see, but knew was there.

Oh well, that's golf.

Marlowe walked up to the green and froze to admire a Gila monster warming itself in the sun. Only the third he'd ever seen, its beaded orange-and-black hide shimmered in the morning light. Strange, he thought. They usually appear only during monsoons, which had come and gone. Entranced, Marlowe felt grateful to be out of Madrid, off dope, and in the presence of such desert royalty. The only problem was La Española, who refused to speak to him. He wondered what she was doing at this very moment back in Spain, her admirers and sycophants lined up and ready for *la marcha* from midnight to dawn, hitting bar after bar, winding up who knows where.

Looking back to the tee, the geezers still hadn't made the turn; probably stopped to grab a bite. As the fat lizard waddled off, Marlowe grabbed a wedge and putter and approached the bunker. Looking down, he found a man lying in the sand, mouth open and staring at the sun. Roughly Marlowe's age, he was dressed in casual Tucson business attire: khaki slacks, blue Levi's shirt, boat shoes, no socks. Marlowe's ball had splashed the sand and rolled next to his ear, an unplayable lie.

"Hey mister, you okay?"

There were no footprints in the trap; someone had carefully raked the entire bunker.

"Hey man, you alright?"

Taking in the frozen eyes, Marlowe watched his chest, but there was no movement. A tarantula hawk wasp hovered close and entered the man's gaping mouth before flying off in search of proper prey.

Dude was dead.

His head spinning, Marlowe panted like a dog and considered his options. As a convicted felon in the state of Arizona, he wanted no part of this—fuck no. Heart racing, he grabbed a 3-iron, went back to the bunker, and tried to retrieve his ball without stepping in the sand; impossible. He looked around for a rake, but whoever had tidied the trap had stashed it somewhere. Staring back at the tee, the foursome had just hit their drives. *Goddamnit!* Marlowe shouldered his bag and headed for the next tee, watching himself from above like a movie he'd heard about, but never seen.

Rushing his drive on 11, Marlowe remembered what his rehab counselor told him about avoiding stressful situations: The smallest little thing could trigger an addict into using again. This here was no trifle; let someone else deal with it. He played the back nine quicker than usual, not bothering to keep score, the image of the corpse flickering in his head.

Coming off 18, he took a look at 10 and noticed a threesome on the green, but everything looked normal. No one ever takes enough club, he thought. That poor dude could go undiscovered for the rest of the day until a hacker skulls a chip across the green and into the bunker. He quickly made his way to the parking lot, put his clubs in the trunk of his '69 Montego, and drove home blasting the AC. It was only at a red light at Kolb and Broadway, when he reached to change the station, that he noticed his hand was shaking. Opening the door to retch, he upchucked a few drops of rancid water and bits of a granola bar he'd eaten for breakfast. A scuzzy biker in the next lane leered, then roared off, leaving Marlowe to choke on his exhaust.

Fuck Tucson, no one gives a shit about nothing.

CHAPTER 2

The body had been in the blazing sun for at least a day; Detective Chavez could smell him from the green above the bunker. The player who found him had probably skulled a chip, the ball skidding across the green and into the trap. Chavez chuckled, playing it out in his mind. Short game is everything; if you can't chip and putt, why bother?

Chavez wiped his brow and looked at the old hacker, huddled with his buddies just off the green. There were footprints in the sand around the corpse, but not much else. He walked over to the foursome, feeling a little bad their round was ruined.

"You're the one who found him, Mister?"

"Name's Floyd. Yeah, I had to play my ball, thought he was just a bum passed out."

"A bum dressed like that? You didn't notice he was dead?"

"Hell, no, there's homeless living here—they use the drinking fountains for water and shit in the toilets, not just javelina and coyotes hanging around. As for his clothes, they get everything donated, don't they? Dress better than I do."

"Why'd you call it in then?"

"Well, my ball was down by his feet, so after I hit a nice little wedge outta the trap, I poked him with my Cleveland, but he didn't move. I called Jack over and told him to put his new goddamn cell phone to use and call 911. We kept playing, but a ranger showed up and asked if we were the ones who found him, told us to come back here to 10. Bad luck to go backwards on a golf course—we want a rain check."

"Those footprints yours?"

"Yeah, I guess, ball was sitting up nice, opened up a 60 and it flew right out."

"Notice anything else when you were down there?"

The old man hesitated, thinking it over.

"Well, yeah, there was a nice, brand-new ball right by his head."

"Where is it?"

The hacker reached into his pocket and handed it over. Chavez used his *abuelo*'s silk monogrammed handkerchief to accept it.

"Why'd you take it? You already played your ball."

"Cause it's a Titleist. I can only afford cheap rocks, no feel."

"How'd your ball get into that back bunker anyway?"

"I skulled a chip, tight lie; should have used a Texas wedge, but I never learn."

Chavez sighed. This was a weird one, and weird ones meant trouble. Victim's driver's license was in his wallet, along with a few twenties and the usual credit cards. George Jenkins, foothills address. Chavez hoped he wasn't related to old man Jenkins, but somehow knew he was. Shit.

"Yeah, it's a hard game if you're stubborn. Okay, sorry about your round, leave your phone numbers with Officer Manning over there in case we have any more questions."

"You think it's murder?"

"No idea, don't talk to anyone about this until you see it in the papers. Even then you're better off staying quiet."

"Can you get us our green fees back, a rain check?"

"You'll have to take that up with the starter, but we're closing the course for the rest of the day."

Keeping it in his *pañuelo* Chavez examined the ball. Titleist 3, marked with a small M written with a red Sharpie. He looked around to see if it could have been an errant shot from another hole, but the 11th tee was adjacent left going off at 90 degrees.

A calling card?

Chavez laughed, he'd been watching too much TV. Thing about police work is each case has its own rhythm, like a golf swing—you can't force it. He took one more look around the green, then nodded to the coroner's assistant to remove the body. Stomach grumbling, he remembered he hadn't eaten all day. If lucky, he'd get a rancid hot dog and a watery Coke in the clubhouse after talking to the staff.

As he walked up the fairway, Chavez noticed all the unrepaired divots, made by the same duffers who complain about bad lies. Golf was a mirror—it revealed everything, warts and all. High above, turkey vultures circled, attracted by the smell. His gut told him a crime had been committed, but how serious he had no idea. A fatalist, Chavez knew it was already solved on a certain level, but whether he would discover the truth was a mystery—it always was.

He wished he could tell Carmen about it, but they were estranged, maybe this time for good. They'd met at Pueblo High, driving up "A" mountain together after class to dream and smooch. He didn't blame her; being involved with a cop was for saints only, and she was anything but. A bilingual kindergarten teacher and community activist, she hid him from her friends, like he was a leper or something. Maybe he was in a sense, losing pieces of his soul bit by bit. It was easier to just go it alone, accept the job for what it was. What did *abuela* used to say?

Ojos que no ven, corazón que no siente . . . what the eyes don't see, the heart doesn't feel.

CHAPTER 3

That evening, Marlowe made sure to catch the local news. He clicked from station to station, but there was no mention of the body in the bunker, only of more hot weather and some pygmy owls causing trouble for developers. He made himself a pasta salad, washed it down with seltzer, then watched an old rerun of *The Rockford Files*. He tried to stay up late to call La Española, catch her before she went to work, but instead went to bed with a copy of Harvey Penick's *Little Red Book*. What could he say to her anyway? That this time was different? That he was sorry she married a junkie? She hated weakness. Her Andalusian mind bristled at the thought of any man begging forgiveness.

Undoubtedly, there was someone else on deck; her beauty demanded attention like a leopard stalking down Las Ramblas. It would be easier for Marlowe's recovery to just walk away, to admit the marriage was doomed from jump street, but something wouldn't let him. There had to be a reason he felt so connected to her, that their lives would only work if they stayed together. He knew she didn't feel that way; it was only her mother who encouraged her to hang on.

He had to win her back.

The one positive Marlowe had going was golf. It was the only thing that pried the monkey off his back and back into its cage. Taking a lesson after a disappointing round, he weakened his grip and started to break 80 regularly, which did wonders for his self-esteem. Most of the desert tracks around Tucson were fairly tight; eliminating one side of the course was the key to scoring low. You can talk to a fade and it lands soft with little roll; a draw won't listen and bounces away. Hackers are slicers who have no idea what a real power fade is. Conversely, they've never turned the ball over in their life, except the occasional duck-hook off the tee. Golf and music had that in common, the vast majority of aficionados sucked playing either one.

Marlowe grew up in Tucson, but split to L.A. after a botched smash-and-grab at a music store. The band soon followed, and playing anytime anywhere for beer, their reputation grew among peers and critics. After cutting a couple half-decent EP's, they found themselves signed to a corrupt but hip label who stole their publishing—but whose fault was that really? Bands will sign anything to make their first real record. At least their name got out there, and after buying a van they hit the road.

Unfortunately, good reviews only get bands so far, and lack of sales meant nonstop touring, which produced a sort of road psychosis. After one particularly brutal two-month marathon, Marlowe returned home to a barking, frightened dog, and his sadly indifferent girlfriend, Robin, who had grown to like it better when he was gone. That led to Marlowe getting fucked-up every night, just like on the road, causing him to write even more depressing songs, resulting in even poorer record sales. Marlowe promised himself things would be different with La Española, but it's a Sid Vicious cycle, with happy endings about as likely as a hole-in-one.

The phone rang, hitting Marlowe like a shot of coke. He jumped out of bed hoping it was her.

"Hello?"

"This Marlowe, Marlowe Billings?"

"Yeah."

"I need to talk to you."

"About what? Who is this?"

"An old friend, can't you guess?"

"Fuckhead Smith? Shithead O'Reilly? It's 11 p.m., what do you want?"

"You have a good game today? Must be nice to play whenever you want."

"Who is this? Grum, is that you? Don't fuck with me, dude."

"No, not Grum, although you haven't been a very good friend to him, have you?"

"Look, you cocksucker, quit playing and tell me what you want."

The phone went dead. Jesus Fucking Christ, as if he didn't have enough on his plate. Marlowe thought about the corpse again, those glassy eyes, the nasty wasp. He quickly got dressed, grabbed his keys, and hopped into the Montego to hit Circle K and score some beer. Breathing hard, he got the key into the ignition, but it wouldn't start. Fuck! He felt like crying, but that took too much effort. He slowly got out of the car and slunked inside, took a long, hot shower, and crawled back into bed.

In the morning he tried the Montego again, and it started right up.

What the hell?

After coffee and a bagel, he went to a meeting, but didn't share and left before the Lord's Prayer. He hated all the hugging; there was only one person he wanted to hold, and she was five thousand miles away.

CHAPTER 4

Forcing himself to miss on the high side, Chavez worked on his routine. He liked to stop at El Rio Golf Course to chip and putt, whenever time allowed. Sinking a left-to-right 8-footer, he snagged the ball and gave it another look. He knew the Titleist was evidence and should be entered as such, but something told him to hold on to it, that it was like a charm and the key to the case. He did have it dusted for prints, but it was spotless from being in the old duffer's pocket.

Chavez knew George Jenkins was a fuck-up, no doubt about it. Foothills brat, in and out of trouble his whole life, real-estate mogul grandfather always bailing him out. The coroner said he'd died of intracerebral hemorrhage, but that didn't explain how he got down in that bunker. There were no footprints besides the old hacker's, which meant someone had raked the trap after the body was dumped there. Either that or they heaved it in, unlikely at best, given George's size and the way he was positioned, like he was taking a snooze. He'd taken a hell of a wallop to the back of his head, like he'd been whacked with a 5-iron, but at this point Chavez had no real way of knowing how he died.

Lined up for another putt, Chavez tried to pinpoint how it all went ugly, and always came back to the coke. It flooded in during the seventies, the Colombians using the Mexicans to ship it north. Before, Tucson was chiefly weed, with black tar heroin piggybacking along. Many legit businesses started with contraband profits: restaurants, construction companies, retail stores, you name it. You got in and out, before law enforcement took notice. Most of it only passed through Tucson, on its way to more lucrative markets. The nickname for Tucson in Sonora was *el almacén*, the warehouse. The dope that did stay was mostly weed, with the tar only in the barrio, poisoning *la raza*.

His own cousin Johnny had overdosed at 16; they'd been best friends. Chavez also liked to get high, but quit after Johnny's funeral. He joined the Air Force, and after a tour in Germany applied to the police academy and got accepted. He advanced quickly, higher-ups liked his Spanish and his ability to get along with uptight Anglos. Making detective, he started in the robbery detail, but soon found himself in homicide, where all the bodies were piling up. It was the cocaine, too much money, and a huge cultural divide between the hyper-ambitious Colombians and the more laid-back Mexicans. Most of the murders went unsolved, carried out by sicarios, stash houses shot up with the neighbors terrified. That never happened before; if a load of weed was lost or stolen, well, you'd make it up next harvest, *no pasa nada*. Now it was like Wall Street or something, ruthless.

It was the last thing Chavez needed: a strange-ass case with lots of media interest. The victim's wealthy family wanted answers. They claimed George had gone straight years ago, was a good father and provider. Word on the street was different: dude had never cleaned up, hung out at strip clubs burning through an eight-ball a day. Pathetic. Dropping the Titleist 3 on the green, Chavez lagged one last putt that rolled in on the last rotation, a lucky ball.

Back in his unmarked Crown Vic, Chavez cranked the AC and headed to Saint Mary's Mexican Food for a red chile burro. Mind churning and stomach growling, he shuffled through the established facts like a deck of cards. Coroner said George's sinuses were shot, but no needle tracks. Blood test came back positive for coke, booze, valium, the usual trifecta. Drugs weren't the reason he died, but Chavez figured his habit was part of the puzzle—it usually was. He'd last been seen by his family at his daughter's school recital, but according to the wife, nothing seemed wrong. That didn't tell him much; addicts were experts at hiding whatever they wanted. As for the wife, he didn't get any guilty vibe, although part of her seemed relieved, which was normal. Chavez didn't hold her lack of emotion against her; she'd been getting ready for this for years now. Marrying a junkie is like loving a snowman—it's gonna melt one way or another, no matter how hard you try to keep it all together.

Chavez kept coming back to the ball. Find whoever had marked that M and chances are he'd find the killer. Why else would someone leave a good Titleist like that? Just didn't make sense. Fucking golfers—superstitious bunch, and usually cheap as hell.

It was a Scottish game after all.

CHAPTER 5

Marlowe knew he shouldn't be going to any bars, but he needed to find Grum. They'd been best friends forever: swim team, Pop Warner football, then tennis at Tucson High, where they got 86'd after taking the team van for a joyride. Grum was the drummer in Marlowe's first band, but quit before they got signed, splitting back to slacker Tucson, where it wasn't so cut-throat. Now he was playing covers at The Boondocks to make the rent, total bummer, but what can a poor boy do?

Turning in at the giant wine bottle out front, Marlowe found a spot for the Montego between two pickups. From the shadows, a voice whispered eight-balls for sale, but Marlowe hated cocaine, even in a speedball. He could just hear the last notes of "Rocky Top" as he entered, the singer saying they'd be back after a short break to a smattering of applause. The light was murky and the air smelled like an aquarium, typical for a swamp-cooled establishment. Grum was at the bar ordering a drink and smoking a cig, looking pretty good, all things considered. He'd just gotten out after a two-year stretch for transporting a load of weed. Marlowe felt guilty for not putting any money on his books, but he'd been strung out in Spain. Grum wouldn't hold it against him though—just not in his nature.

"Very funny fucker, how'd you know I was back?"

Grum spun around, ready to strike with that mongoose right hand of his.

"Marlowe fucking Billings! What happened? That Spanish princess give you the boot?"

Grum quit smiling when he saw Marlowe's reaction.

"Dude, I'm sorry—really? Things not working out?"

"Let's go sit down, I'll tell ya all about it."

"Sure, sure, you wanna a drink?"

"No, I'm good, on the wagon."

"Not walking that 12-step pier I hope—Jimmy, put it on my tab."

Grum put his arm around Marlowe's shoulder and led him to a booth by the stage. A few couples were dancing to the jukebox, Dolly singing "Jolene".

"You call me last night, Grum? No fucking around."

"Hell no, didn't even know you were back—shit, I just got out myself."

"Yeah I know, someone in a meeting filled me in. Sorry I never wrote you."

"Meeting? Not you too, brother? It's worse than Scientology."

"I'm no convert, just need to get off the dope, can't have it all."

"I hear you, brother. I did a lot of thinking locked up. Lost everything, the house, Julie, everything. Is it over with you and her? I can never pronounce her name."

"Dunno, maybe. She's still in Madrid, hopefully with her legs closed, but I wouldn't be surprised."

"Ah fuck, we ain't kids anymore. Shit hurts. You going back to Spain?"

"I don't trust myself, dope is everywhere. The whole country is strung out on Afghan brown."

"But dude, what about here? This is Tucson, remember?"

"Yeah, but for some reason I don't associate it with heroin. Beer and weed, sure, but I never had a habit here. It's all psychological I guess. I know the streets are paved with tar but . . ."

A skinny mestizo with long hair and dilated eyes shuffled over to tell Grum they were on in five.

"Marlowe, you know Louie, right? Louie Soto?"

"Hey Louie, love your playing, nice to see you again."

"Same here, Marlowe—let me know if you ever need a guitar player. This bar life is killing me. I want to play those summer festivals in Europe."

"It ain't much better over there, buddy."

"I'd love to find out, call me anytime well. I'm way better than the güero surfer boy you got—that dude never finishes a lead."

Marlowe laughed as Louie hit up a cute foothills housewife, out slumming with the flatlanders. He whispered something nasty in her ear as she licked her lips in anticipation.

"Okay, Grum, I gotta split before I get a haircut. You play golf anymore?"

"Nah man, I always sucked, remember? Takes too much time—would rather see a movie or play some racquetball like Elvis. Speaking of golf, you remember George Jenkins? Dad was that rich developer?"

"Not really, he went to Tucson High?"

"No Salpointe, I met him there after I got kicked out of Tucson. I used to buy blow from him. Anyway, they found him dead on a golf course—coroner says it's suspicious."

Marlowe tried to remain calm, was Grum testing him?

"Murder? They know who did it?"

"Nope, but word is an old friend of ours is mixed up in it."

"Nestor? Thought he was locked up in California?"

"No, he's out, but it's all gossip right now—you know how Tucson is. Don't be a stranger, brother. Let me know if you need any weed when you get your mojo back."

Marlowe took a piss, then walked out the back door to the band kicking it off with some Skynyrd.

Ooh, ooh that smell, can't you smell that smell?

A patrol car was parked in the adjacent lot, watching who was going in and out. Feeling paranoid, Marlowe drove carefully home, as if he'd done something terribly wrong, something besides just being born. What the fuck was he doing back here anyway? Loserville. Searching for a station, an old regional hit filled the Montego with a soaring melody.

Gotta see the lights of Tucson, gotta pack, c'mon get a move on.

CHAPTER 6

Waking to the siren of an ambulance, it took Marlowe a few seconds to remember where he was. He got up and made some coffee, then took a nice greasy shit with clean breakage, a minor miracle. He loved having his mornings back, the best part of the day if you're clean and sober.

He hopped on a mountain bike and took a spin through Mo Udall Park, then across Tanque Verde Road to the neighborhood where he'd grown up. It felt strange being back, but when his L.A. stuntman brother offered him the use of his vacant townhouse, well, he couldn't pass it up. Back in '67, when the family arrived from California, this was the edge of town. Indian Ridge was an affordable semi-custom home subdivision populated with middle-class professionals: accountants, teachers, dentists, small-business owners. Adjacent was lawyer, banker, and old-money–infested Tucson Country Club Estates, the class divide.

Coming to Topke Street, Marlowe hung a left and went down memory lane. The low-slung ranch homes and desert-friendly landscaping had hardly changed at all. He and his friends had run riot here, riding dirt bikes and smoking pot, blowing up mailboxes, boning chicks from the hated enclave to the west. He'd left home on Father's Day after an altercation with the old man, but Marlowe was an insufferable teenager and should have been kicked out at puberty. He stopped to gander at his old burnt adobe house, with its two majestic palm trees in the front yard. Marlowe felt whimsical, and half expected his younger self to come outside and flip him off. An older Volvo station wagon was parked in the carport, a good indication the neighborhood hadn't changed much, still full of professors and plumbers.

Coasting downhill to Sabino Canyon Road, Marlowe passed the still protected archeological site where there'd been an ancient Indian settlement. Finding pottery shards and arrowheads was a normal occurrence when he was a kid, along with critters like tarantulas and horny toads. In his recent walks behind Mo Udall Park, Marlowe had yet to see either of the latter—where did they all go? Only the coyotes remained, feasting on rabbits and rock squirrels, with the occasional cat or poodle a special treat.

Lost in the past, Marlowe pedaled home, depressed that after a decade he was back with nothing to show except a few marginal records and a wayward wife. He stopped to watch some kids jump off the high dive at Udall Pool, facing down their fear. He'd been given a second chance; he could wallow in the mire, or face the future and find a new hustle. Maybe go back to college, learn to write something legit, like a novel or a decent poem. Rock 'n' roll was for kids, not a thirty-year-old junkie. Maybe if he got it together, La Española would fall in love with him for real, not the fame-fucking groupie shit that attracted her to him in the first place.

Tired from the ride, Marlowe put the bike away, but felt someone behind him in the street. Taking a peek, it was just a roadrunner giving him the stink-eye. He chuckled and went inside, putting his mouth under the kitchen faucet to guzzle the piped-in Colorado River swill that tasted like chlorine, a far cry from the refreshing groundwater of his youth. Well, at least the taps were still running—but for how long? He picked up the phone to check his voicemail, hoping for a message from Spain, but instead got a chill down his spine.

"Marlowe, Marlowe fucking Billings. This is Nestor—remember me, amigo? We need to talk, and soon. Don't make me go find you, homie, I ain't playing. Meet me at Pico De Gallo on South 4th tomorrow at noon—gives you plenty of time to golf in the morning. Yeah, I know all about you playing that faggot rich white-boy's game. Tasty fish tacos, dude, and the salsa is rocket fuel. Okay pues, hasta pronto, don't let me down."

Head spinning, Marlowe just made it back to the sink to heave. It was the same voice as before—why hadn't he recognized it? Nestor was the last person he wanted to see; everything he touched went bad one way or another. They'd been friends once, but Nestor had crossed over to the dark side, and no way could Marlowe hang with that. Lifting his head, he stared at a Fritz Scholder print of a gaunt Indian cowboy holding a can of Coors, like death itself. Marlowe's nose dripped snot, why the fuck was this shit happening? First the corpse and now Nestor, coming back to fuck his life up for good.

Splashing his face with water, he rinsed the sink of watery puke, watching it circle the drain before disappearing down into the void.

That night, Marlowe dreamed he smoked some weed and felt unbelievably sad, like he'd committed a grave sin. He woke with a start and realized he was still sober; everything was okay. Maybe that's all he had to do—not use like the old-timers said, one day at a time. Insomnia cursed, he picked up a *Golf Digest* and read a profile of Tiger Woods, still a teenager but surely the next sensation. He wondered what that was like, reading about how great you would be in the future. Having been a bright, precocious child himself, Marlowe knew how debilitating such expectations could be, and hoped Tiger would not implode before he'd even started.

He gave it 50/50.

CHAPTER 7

The next morning, pretending it mattered, Marlowe hit his knees and prayed that Nestor was only fucking with him. After breakfast, he took a long walk through the desert and almost felt the serenity that other addicts were always going on about.

Fake it till you make it.

Oddly calm, Marlowe enjoyed the drive to the southside, listening to norteño corridos on the AM radio. Tucsonans and *tucsonenses* alike love their Mexican music, but also its food, and Pico De Gallo was one of the best taquerias around. He found Nestor in a back corner, enjoying a *raspado* from next door and looking exactly the same as ever, *apuesto*. He got up and gave Marlowe a hug, holding him a little too tight for a little too long, smelling faintly of tobacco and creosote.

"What, you already eat?"

"Sometimes I like *postre* first, satisfy my sweet tooth. Go order us some tacos and horchata. Tell Jaime to put it on my tab."

Marlowe walked to the counter feeling light, like he wasn't really here. He remembered the owner, Jaime, from way back, acting nervous as he took the order. When told to put it on Nestor's tab, he just waved his hand that all was good. Waiting patiently, in no hurry, Marlowe watched the cook ball up some masa in her palm before putting it in a tortilladora to flatten, then placing it on the hot comal to cook. Yum.

Taking it all back on a tray, Marlowe tried to stay cool. Nestor was a shark; if he smelled fear he would rip you apart. He first came around the band house a decade past, and was accepted like anyone else. This Nestor never forgot, Marlowe and Grum not caring where he'd been or what he'd done, a murderer at age 15. One night, everyone high on Quaaludes, he told them all about it. He didn't want to shoot, but the fucker was after a pound of weed Nestor kept stashed in his closet. Respect was everything in the barrio; he had to stand his ground. Hand shaking, Nestor squeezed the trigger, the bullet severing an artery in the dude's neck. He took off, leaving the poor bastard to bleed to death. He spent a week on the streets, before being picked up and sentenced to juvie gladiator school up in Phoenix. Released at 18, he got into the punk scene and started hitting shows, where they all met soon enough.

"What happened with your Spanish señorita? She get tired of your gringo ass?"

"I don't wanna talk about it."

Nestor started to sing . . .

"I don't want to talk about it, how you broke my heart."

"What about your frenchy? I always liked her."

"She's back in L.A., we had a kid."

"Congratulations, you a good dad?"

"To tell the truth, I hate babies, shitting and crying all the time."

"That's what they do."

Marlowe squirted some salsa on a taco and took a bite. Holy fuck, glorious. Eyes pinned, Nestor stuck with his *raspado*.

"So how come you always ignore me, Marlowe? Ain't we friends?"

"Nestor, I told you back in L.A. how it is. Your lifestyle makes it impossible. I can't catch another case, and I never know what you're up to. You're dangerous to be around, and you meet people through me who you exploit to your benefit."

"Like who? That's bullshit."

"Erica, Riley, Jonathan—should I go on?"

Nestor stared hard at Marlowe. He didn't like it, but the dudens always talked straight. He loved these punk white boys—they were the closest thing he had to family.

"I know you found that body, Marlowe."

Marlowe kept chewing but couldn't swallow.

"A friend of mine works out there. He's a *mojado* that got into it with some *polleros*. I helped straighten it out. He was watching, waiting for someone to find poor George."

"How did he know it was me?"

"He took a look at the starter's sheet, your name was top of the list."

"So why would he tell you about it?"

"Because I told him to keep watch."

Stunned, Marlowe could hardly believe what he was hearing. None of it made sense—what were the fucking odds? Again, he felt like he was watching himself in a film, that none of this was real.

"You kill him?"

"Let's just say Georgie boy finally ran out of luck."

"Why are you telling me this?"

"The Nogales plaza is up for grabs. Sinaloa wants it back."

"So what?"

"You make a good distraction, homie. A white boy decoy to mess shit up."

"Decoy? For who?"

"That's the question, right? Who can you trust?"

Nestor finished his *raspado* and dug into his tacos, then took a sip of his horchata and burped.

"Don't worry, Marlowe, ain't nothing gonna happen."

"Nestor, you just made me an accessory after the fact, what the fuck?"

"Sorry, pues, I had to. It'll all make sense later, trust me."

Nestor got up, leaving Marlowe to clean off the table.

"You want a little *chiva* to take the edge off?"

Marlowe held Nestor's gaze for a long second before shaking his head no.

"Okay, mi carnal, be a saint—just remember what they say in those rooms: one day at a time, live and let live, more will be revealed."

Nestor waltzed off like he'd just cashed a check. Marlowe pushed his tacos away and stared at a picture on the wall: a Yaqui Deer Dancer bringing forth the Flower World. Nowadays, they rarely sacrificed a deer during ceremonies, but still danced all night to bring harmony to a chaotic world. Tourists were tolerated, but never encouraged at the poverty-stricken reservations located right in the city.

Out the front door, Marlowe watched Nestor drive off in an old pickup, with a bright yellow "The Thing" bumper sticker. Fucker might be evil, but he had a wicked sense of humor.

CHAPTER 8

Detective Chavez took a last frozen bite of a mango paleta and watched Nestor come out of Pico De Gallo and head to his truck. Now he had to make a decision: follow him or wait for his Anglo friend. The owner, Jaime, had called an hour before, told him Nestor García was back in town, had returned like a nasty toe fungus. Chavez was related to Jaime through his aunt, they had a deal that Jaime would be a *halcón*, his lookout. Everyone loves a good fish taco, and Pico De Gallo was like South Tucson central.

Cursing he didn't get the truck's plate, Chavez decided to wait. Nestor was too smart to tail anyway. There was cartel trouble in Nogales, and Chavez figured Nestor's reappearance had something to do with it, and maybe his pal as well. Jaime said the güero was wearing a T-shirt, Bermuda shorts, flip-flops, the usual Tucson slacker uniform.

Sure enough, the gringo soon followed and got into an old classic Mercury. He headed north on 6th to 22nd Street before hanging a right. Chavez stayed back a few cars, but could tell this guy was oblivious to being followed, most likely a regular Joe. He called in the plate and it came back clean, registered to one Marlowe Billings. Of course he couldn't be sure of the driver's identity, but he did match the registrant's height and weight. He wondered what the dude's connection to Nestor was, a very bad actor who Chavez had wanted to put away for years, going back to a drug rip-off gone bad. The buyer took a shotgun blast to the face, losing his vision. Nestor was the shooter, but Chavez couldn't prove it; victim refused to testify, a typical turn of events.

Pulling into a two-story office complex just past Plumer, Chavez watched the subject go up the stairs to where a few people were hanging around on the landing having a smoke. Chavez knew this was a recovery meeting spot; it wasn't the first time he tailed someone here. Attendance was often mandatory, part of parole or probation, but just because you were in a meeting didn't mean shit. Twelve-step groups were the same as any other organization or church—plenty of hypocrites and liars.

Chavez parked in the shade and took a nap, figuring it'd be an hour at least. He woke up thirty minutes later and watched the subject come back down the stairs and into his car. Chavez looked up at the door but no one else was coming out; dude had left early. The Montego made a right out of the parking lot and kept heading east on 22nd, before taking a left on Alvernon Way and on down to Randolph Golf Course.

Watching the gringo take his clubs out of the trunk, Chavez grinned. Cases had their own internal logic—he learned that long ago. He wasn't exactly surprised the guy was a golfer, but still it made him happy. He thought about the body out at Fred Enke, Nestor being back in town, the big ball of confusion as The Temptations sang—chaos theory. He knew most likely there was no connection, but still felt satisfied on some deep level. Making a split decision, he got out and grabbed his own sticks from the trunk, then sat on the Crown Vic's bumper to change shoes while watching the güero do the same.

Metal spikes crunching on the asphalt, Chavez followed him to the starter's booth and put his name on the list right below, yes, Marlowe Billings. He'd run the name later, see if he had a record or currently on probation. The starter mumbled there was just a few reservations in front, and he'd probably be on the tee in fifteen minutes. Chavez handed him a fiver, said to make sure to put him and Billings together.

Chavez went into the pro shop to pay his green fees, then stroked a few practice putts while watching Marlowe do the same. Names soon announced over the PA, they found themselves as a twosome on the first tee. Shaking hands the way golfers do, they introduced themselves using first names only, part of the code. The worst thing you could do when playing with a stranger was to ask too many questions, like what someone did for a living, or where they lived. On the course, everyone was equal—that is if you could play a little.

Chavez nodded for Marlowe to tee off first, and noticed he pulled out a fairway wood, smart move. He watched him find a Sharpie in his bag, mark his ball and a backup, then smack a nice little draw out there about 200 yards. Chavez went for it with his driver and pushed it a little right, but had only 150 left from the rough. They shouldered their bags, just heading off when a middle-aged fatty appeared, huffing and puffing with a huge pro-type bag on a fancy pull cart.

"Fellas, fellas, hold on, the starter told me to join you."

Chavez and Marlowe turned around and sighed, too good to be true.

The hacker put on a brand-new glove, took a few ugly practice swings with an expensive driver, then hit a worm burner out about a 100 yards, but at least it was straight.

"Thanks, guys—name's Casper, just like the ghost."

They all made their way down the fairway separated by several yards—no one wants to be crowded on the course. Chavez and Marlowe stopped to the right of where the duffer's drive wound up, and waited for him to catch up. The plumper took out a 3-iron, then hit a dead pull that bounded into the trees up by the green. Chavez looked at Marlowe, who returned his disgusted look; this guy was gonna slow down and fuck up their round for sure. He sported a grand worth of gear, but had probably never taken a lesson in his life. At his level, all he had to do was hit a 5-iron off the tee, then a 7 down the fairway, a 9-iron onto the green, two putt, and he would have his bogey.

Unfortunately, the worse the golfer, the less common sense.

Chavez watched as Marlowe found his ball in a divot, but didn't move it to improve his lie. Instead, he gripped down on a short iron, the ball well back in his stance, and smacked a textbook knock-down that came out of the divot low and hot, winding up about ten yards from the green. Sweet. Chavez's own ball was sitting up nice in the first cut, and he hit a routine little 8-iron to the center of the green, ignoring the sucker back left pin. The hacker miraculously "found" his ball in a clearing and managed to hit the lower green with his pitching wedge. Next in turn, Marlowe clipped a long chip that landed just on the green and rolled to about 5 feet below the hole, marking his ball with a dime. The hacker lagged a long putt to about 3 feet shy, promptly giving himself the putt while stepping on Marlowe's line. Shaking his head, Chavez played it safe with his own putt, leaving himself a foot and a half, which he finished up for par. Carefully replacing his ball, Marlowe stroked a firm putt but got horse-shoed. He tapped it in, then made room for Chavez, who replaced the flag. Walking to the next tee, the fatty couldn't help providing commentary.

"Two bogeys and a par, not a bad start, gentlemen!"

Chavez gave Marlowe a wry look, who returned it with a shrug.

"Gonna be a long round, you playing 18?"

"No, snuck out from work, gotta get back before five."

"Well, I probably won't get 18 in with this guy, already a half-hole behind, glad we got hackers behind us as well. Clowns to the left of me, jokers to the right . . ."

Chavez laughed and finished the lyric . . .

"Stuck in the fairway with you."

Observing his demeanor on the course, Chavez found himself liking this Marlowe Billings. Gringo played by the rules, no mulligans, took his medicine after hitting a bad shot, didn't try any miraculous recoveries. He was even polite to the duffer, encouraging him when appropriate. Chavez pondered what his connection to Nestor was—extortion? Unlikely, given his actions. Who goes to play golf after being threatened? Once again, the mystery of Anglos hit him, their cold Protestant reasoning so different from his own fatalistic Mexican upbringing.

They finally arrived at the 9th green, where Chavez congratulated Marlowe for making a 12-footer. Holding the flag, he reached into the hole to get Marlowe's ball, but accidentally dropped it by his foot. He bent over to get it, and noticed the mark, a small M in red ink, right below Titleist 3 in black. No fucking way. Chavez looked up and tossed it back.

"Nice meeting you, Marlowe. Hope to play with you again."

They all shook hands, and as the duffer and Marlowe walked off toward the 10th tee, Chavez stood frozen in wonder by the side of the green. A loud "foooore!" rang out. Chavez instinctively ducked before a ball bounced off the cart path and whizzed by his head. He gave a wave of peace to the group behind, then abruptly turned and headed for the parking lot, fingering the San Miguel medallion he wore around his neck.

What were the fucking odds?

CHAPTER 9

B ack at the townhouse, Marlowe put on his trunks and headed down to the small community pool no one ever used. Water warm from the sun, he floated on his back, staring at the sky just starting to darken. He thought of La Española back in Spain, was she was out partying till dawn, tipsy from cava and cocaine, thinking about who she would go home and fuck? He'd never really trusted her; it was like hoping a bag of dope left in a dive bar would never get snatched. In a way, she *was* like heroin to him—like Jeffrey Lee sang—and cannot miss a vein.

As a matter of routine, just like he did in his own backyard pool as a kid, Marlowe checked all the filter baskets before leaving. In one, he found a zebra-tailed lizard, half-drowned clinging to the side. He gently picked it up, placing it on the cool decking to recover. Shuddering for a few seconds, it scurried off to the shelter of a prickly pear. Marlowe felt jealous of its reality: nothing to think about, argue over, dream, or imagine. Just stimulus and response, pure survival. Humans were the only animals terrorized by their own existence, fear analyzed and internalized, fight or flight manifested as depression, neurosis, violence, and addiction. No wonder God had to be invented, and houses of worship built to keep it all at bay.

Marlowe walked home in the darkness and thought about Nestor dragging him into this mess, what to believe and what was bullshit. The illegal out at Fred Enke—was that really true? The Nogales plaza back in play—what would a spoiled country-club brat like George know about that? And why was Nestor out of prison anyway—wasn't there a three-strike rule that got you life? None of it made sense, the coincidences too hard to believe.

That night lying in bed, Marlowe thumbed through an old *Penthouse* hoping he could rub one out, but he couldn't get hard. He soon gave up, and got out a notebook to write her a letter.

Mi Querida,

How can I begin to explain to you how I feel? How can I tell you how much your love means to me? These are just words I'm writing, the effort put forth worth little, the actions behind them what counts. I have been going to meetings to try to figure it all out, to understand why I have to live life with a buffer between myself and reality. They call it a disease but I'm not so sure, I think it has more to do with a lack of faith that life is worth living, that to be born is a magical thing to be cherished and celebrated, not denigrated and maligned. I've been trying to get in shape physically, hoping that helps my mental condition, which goes from happy to sad like a teenager. I think of you every minute, and realize that my behavior perhaps can never be forgiven. This is the hardest part, to accept that even if I regain my sanity, I will still never feel your touch again, never hear you sigh once more in pleasure. My god, what have I done? I ask that every day.

Forever yours,

Marlowe

Putting the letter in the nightstand, he turned off the light and prayed for sleep. In rehab, they said insomnia was part of the process and wouldn't kill you, but Marlowe wasn't so sure. Only the image of hanging from a tree or jumping off a bridge gave him peace. Outside, coyotes made a kill, yapping in joy. Marlowe wished he was closer to downtown, so he could hear a train. He finally drifted off to the neighbors arguing about money, the woman reduced to tears, the man slamming doors in a drunken rage.

CHAPTER 10

Chavez dreaded meeting the old man, but knew he couldn't avoid him any longer. Turning left off Tanque Verde and entering Tucson Country Club, he stopped at the guard house to give his name. The rent-a-cop looked down at him and sneered, total asshole. Chavez had been here a few times before, a robbery and a drug overdose, and always felt like a cheap suit in a tuxedo factory. Blacks and Jews were not allowed to own property here, and even after redlining became illegal, the real-estate agents still found a way. Hispanics could buy—maybe if you were a rich Cuban doctor or something, but that was about it. Taking a left on Miramar from Camino Principal, he could see the beautiful golf course hiding between the gorgeous low-slung custom homes, but he'd never seen anyone playing.

Finding the address, he turned into a long circular driveway and parked behind a sun-faded Corolla, probably the maid. Ringing the doorbell, he waited for what seemed like hours before the door opened to a woman's face that he recognized but couldn't quite place.

"Raymond, Raimundo? Is that you?"

Momentarily flustered, Chavez stared at the middle-aged woman in jeans and T-shirt, holding a duster.

"Soy Marta, tu vecina, me recordaste?"

Chavez smiled with the sweet memory of galletas and chocolate milk being offered after doing yard work for her.

"Of course I remember you, Marta, cómo estás? And Miguel?"

Marta smiled, then frowned.

"Miguel ya se murió, the cancer got him. He wouldn't go to the doctor, said God would decide."

"Oh, I'm sorry, Marta—really I am. Is El Jefe home? I have an appointment for two o'clock."

"Sí, sí, he told me an official was coming, but I didn't know it would be you. Let me show you the way."

Walking behind her, Chavez noticed her jeans were designer and tennis shoes expensive—at least he's paying her okay. The home was furnished with mid-century pieces, probably bought new back in the day. He felt himself getting smaller, the shame of growing up poor and Mexican returning. This made him angry, and as she knocked on the study's door he felt like barging in, with badge out and gun drawn. Marta seemed to notice and touched his arm reassuringly; finally a sandpaper voice called for them to come in.

"Detective Chavez, hello, please take a seat. Marta, could you bring us some lemonade—would that suit you, Detective?"

"Yes, thank you, a little iced tea splashed in if you could."

"Good idea—two Arnold Palmers, Marta, thank you."

Chavez sat down in front of the rustic hand-carved wooden desk. It looked ancient, older even than Mr. Jenkins who sat behind it. The walls had Remingtons and Indian art, kachina dolls on tables, an old shotgun over the fireplace. Typical old-school Southwestern money.

"I made a few inquiries about you, Detective. My friends in the department say you're quite capable."

Chavez took in the old man, his face all bone, almost like a white sugar-skull with dark green eyes. He was very thin, wearing a wool cardigan to shield from the air-conditioning. Chavez guessed about six-two if not taller.

"I try to do my duty—I'm sorry for the events that have brought me here."

"Let's not beat around the bush, Detective—my grandson was a degenerate. I'm not surprised this has happened—the circumstances around his murder, yes, but not that he finally met his fate."

"Do you know anyone who would want him dead?"

The old man sighed and looked out a window with a view of a perfectly manicured fairway. A solitary golfer with an old Black caddie was getting ready for his approach shot, and they both waited for him to swing as if they were a respectful gallery. Marta knocked gently on the door and brought in their drinks, then left without a word.

"Do you know how I made my money, Detective?"

"I assume through real-estate development, Mr. Jenkins. The city has doubled in size in just my lifetime, and you were here almost at the beginning."

"Yes, I was born the same year Arizona became a state, 1912. My father was a merchant, owned a general store, came out from Boston. He brought with him his new bride, my mother, but she died of consumption after having me and my two sisters. I was ten."

"Tough age to lose a mother."

They both sipped their drinks and looked out the window again, but the fairway was empty now.

"My father was only thirty and wanted more children, but there were few suitable women here—white women that is. Instead, he did something common for the day—he took a common-law wife, a Mexican gal who'd lost her husband in a mining accident. I never knew this, of course; he kept both households firmly apart. I only found out later I had a half-brother and sister, long story. Unfortunately, my father was a gambler—he had a decadent streak like my grandson George, and when he died both families were left destitute. I was the oldest, and the responsibility fell on me to keep the Anglo side going."

Chavez knew enough to stay quiet. The old man was spilling his guts, no different than a crackhead handcuffed to a desk in an interrogation room.

"First thing I had to do was clear my father's debts, and fortunately most of his creditors were quite reasonable when apprised of the circumstances. But there was this one individual—I cannot tell you his name for obvious reasons—he wanted us all broken up and put in the poorhouse. He resented the Anglo invasion, as he put it. That I could not agree to, so I took care of it in the fashion of the day."

Chavez stared hard at the old man who had just admitted to murder.

"I'm not proud of it, but it had to be done. I knew in my heart that someday I would pay, in one way or another, and that time is now with the demise of my grandson. All of my wealth, the life that my children and grandchildren enjoy, is because of that choice I made. I tried to make something great out of a mortal sin, but we both know that's impossible, don't we, Detective?"

Chavez didn't like this one bit, playing priest in the confessional for this living cadaver. It was the same old shit, a white man asking a brown for forgiveness, pretending he was the victim in this unjust world.

"What does this have to do with my case?"

"Because I think it's related—that whoever killed George knows what I did all those years ago."

"How?"

"That I can't tell you, at least not yet. I have other people to worry about. Yes, George got what was coming to him, and maybe I will, too, but I want the rest of my family to be protected from this sordid business."

"Understood, but bear in mind if through my investigation I gather evidence to prosecute you for your past actions I will."

"I would expect nothing less."

Chavez took another sip of the delicious brew and rolled the dice.

"Have you ever heard the name Marlowe Billings?"

The old man looked up with a start.

"Why, yes I do. That was the rascal who got one of my granddaughters pregnant; she later terminated the pregnancy at my insistence. Why do you ask—is he involved?"

"It's just a hunch, nothing solid yet. Here's my card, Mr. Jenkins. If you decide to fully cooperate, don't hesitate to call. You're playing with fire, but I won't lecture. In Spanish we say *a lo pecho, hecho.*"

"Yes, take heart, what's done is done. I wish I could, Detective, but I'm too old to ask for mercy."

On the way out, Chavez stopped to give Marta a hug and whispered in her ear.

"If you know anything about George, call me. Podríamos prevenir otra tragedia, stop anyone else from getting killed."

Leaving, he noticed a white tradesman van in the driveway. The driver was just getting out, a toolbelt in hand. Chavez nodded but got a blank stare back, fucking cracker jailbird. The front door opened and Marta called out.

"Roy, Mr. Jenkins would like to talk to you right away."

Old man keeps funny company, Chavez thought. What's so urgent?

CHAPTER 11

Up early, Marlowe jumped in the Montego to clear his mind. Heading east, he stopped at Mail Boxes Etc. to send the letter to La Española, then drove out where a Beatle had a big spread. Marlowe liked Harrison the best, who wrestled with the metaphysical, while Paul was the overachieving wonder boy. John was the cool asshole, murdered when he finally embraced his own humanity. Ringo was the mascot, but the others loved him, and every band needs someone to protect. Families are no different, Marlowe thought; they break up when assigned roles are challenged or abandoned.

He took a left on Soldier Trail, right on Roger, entered Agua Caliente Park, and parked by the old ranch house. Marlowe hardly noticed the white van behind him, the only other vehicle around. He got out, strolled over to the spring-fed oasis, and imagined life a century past. Native tribes were here much longer, but no one really chooses to live in the desert. Someone, somewhere, had pushed you here. Great Depression lungers came on doctor's orders, Midwestern businessmen fleeing competition and regulation, rich divorcees tired of the gossip back east searching for one last fling. Even the mafia took refuge here, crazy old Joe Bonanno and shrewd Pete Licavoli soaked up the sun as indictments rained down in Brooklyn and Detroit.

Immigrants all.

Walking the nature path past the pond, he came upon a pack of Harris Hawks hunting on the ground. They surrounded a large prickly pear, and waited for their prey to be flushed out. Marlowe stayed still, not believing his luck. The smallest of the cast darted into the thorns, and a rock squirrel scrambled out to be nabbed by sharp talons.

He shuddered imagining the terror of the prey, but nature was honest and nothing could diminish its brutality. Thinking of Nestor and the corpse, Marlowe decided to call the cops and tell them all he knew. Fuck this criminal shit; he had enough to worry about just staying clean. If Nestor caught another case, too bad—that wasn't his fault, and if he came after him, well, he would just have to take that chance. He wouldn't snitch—hell, he didn't know how George died anyway, but he wasn't gonna be the fall guy either, or a goddamn gringo decoy, as Nestor put it.

Marlowe felt relieved heading back to his car. Maybe it *was* like what they said in the rooms: just do the next right thing, don't worry about a future you can't control. He stuck the key in the door, but was interrupted before he got in.

"Mister? Could you help me with a jump?"

Marlowe turned and saw a guy in painter whites holding jumper cables next to his van parked a few spaces down.

"Sure, how ya wanna do it?"

The man approached with a weird grin.

"Ah, thanks. I just replaced the battery, but the summer heat fries them. Maybe you back up and park facing me, and we can push my van into the right position?"

"Sounds like a plan."

Turning back around to open his door, Marlowe was blinded by an explosion inside his head accompanied by a deafening roar, then sweet nothing.

CHAPTER 12

Chavez admired the U of A campus, although he never attended. He often wondered what life would be like if he'd never joined the Air Force, then TPD. He respected academics and scientists, was fascinated by it all. He certainly had the grades to go to college, but money was tight in the Chavez household. His dad acted angry when he first signed up, but Chavez knew he was secretly relieved. Carmen encouraged him to get a law degree, but he hardly had any free time as it was.

Entering the beautiful new library with its large windows, Chavez watched students playing frisbee on the mall, with the gorgeous Catalinas in the distance. Reluctantly turning away, he found the media section and showed his badge to a friendly looking librarian typing on a computer at her desk.

"Afternoon, ma'am. Detective Chavez, Tucson Police Department. I'm interested in any newspaper articles of unsolved local homicides, roughly from 1930 to 1935."

"Oh my, that's a long time ago. We do have all Tucson newspapers on microfiche going back to the last century, but you'll have to dig through them one by one."

"That's fine, if you could just show me how to operate the viewer and bring me the film, I would very much appreciate it."

"How exciting. Let me just save what I was doing and I'll be right with you."

Chavez watched her insert a floppy disk into a tower and make the necessary keystrokes. He knew this was the future, but it gave him anxiety. With computers he was unsure of what would happen in a new reality, how criminals could hide inside systems, with no way to trace them. Maybe reality itself would change. He didn't know what that would look like, but it made him nervous. The librarian soon led him to an area with about a dozen microfiche readers set up in rows, half occupied.

"You know it's too bad we're not doing this a decade from now, then everything will be on a searchable database. You'll just type some keywords and a search engine will find the relevant information."

"Yes, the World Wide Web."

"That should make your ability to solve crimes much easier."

"Really? I'm not so sure."

After bringing a stack of film and showing him how to work the viewer, the librarian left him to it. Chavez found himself lost in the past, reading the *Arizona Daily Star* hoping to find any cases that lined up with the old man's story. He tried to stay focused, but couldn't resist articles about daily life. He was surprised to learn that El Rio Golf Course used to be a private country club, and the El Conquistador Hotel was first located where El Con Mall is now. Not surprisingly, there were few stories about his own community, as if Hispanics didn't exist in what had only recently been Mexico. One headline caught his eye, buried three pages deep:

Tavern Owner Shot

A barrio businessman was shot, after closing his bar this Saturday evening past. Eusebio Pérez was found by a passing motorist on South Meyer Street around midnight, suffering from a gunshot wound to the chest. Mr. Pérez is currently at Saint Mary's Hospital after emergency surgery. Police say they have no suspects at this time, and anyone with information should contact Tucson Police Department immediately.

Then two days later . . .

Local Proprietor Dies From Assault

A barrio tavern owner shot last Saturday evening has died after emergency surgery on Sunday. Eusebio Pérez had just closed for the night when accosted by an unknown assailant. Found by a passerby, the victim reportedly never regained

consciousness after surgery. Police are asking the community for any information
they may have regarding this heinous act, anonymity guaranteed.

Chavez felt a tingle. He made copies of the articles, thanked the librarian, then hit an Eegee's on the way back to the office. As he ate, he thought about Jenkins and his story. Tucson once belonged to Spain, then Mexico, but a huge part of that history was destroyed when a convention center was built downtown in the late '60s. An entire Mexican barrio had been razed to make "urban renewal" happen, and the Jenkins real-estate company was deeply involved. Chavez never understood it—there was plenty of empty land for the convention center nearby; why wipe out an entire community's heart and soul?

Now it all made sense—the old man was covering up for his crime, subconsciously or otherwise. He had family downtown, legally recognized maybe not, but his own flesh and blood thrown out of their homes and businesses. Jenkins and his fellow "boosters" were ashamed of Tucson's Mexican heritage. They built a fake western amusement park outside the city, while destroying an actual living neighborhood that Hollywood had frequently used for old Mexico. Refusing to enforce health and building codes, they let it deteriorate so they could justify their actions. Typical gringo behavior.

Thinking of Carmen, Chavez understood why her anger simmered like it did. He'd spent years putting people in jail, often from his own community. Maybe he *was* a traitor, just like she said. It all made him angry, and more than a little sad. He pulled out a bottle of tequila from his desk and splashed some in his lemon Eegee's. These goddamn Anglos write the laws and never seem to wind up in jail for the crimes they commit. When was the tide gonna turn, if ever?

He wanted his pueblo back.

CHAPTER 13

Marlowe woke in darkness, thirsty and nauseous. A peach-pit sized lump was oozing blood from the back of his skull. Eyes adjusting, he could barely make out the inside panel doors of a van, along with a commercial paint sprayer, buckets, and the drop cloth he was lying on. He remembered driving out to Agua Caliente Park, but that was it.

He forced himself up, crawled to the door, felt for a latch, and gave it a push. To his relief it opened right up, revealing the end of a driveway leading to a putting green. An old man practiced his chipping, while a workman in painter's whites was up on a ladder trimming a mesquite with loppers. They both noticed Marlowe, paused at the same time, then went back to their activities.

Marlowe thought it a dream, and walked toward them. He opened a little wooden gate to an emerald carpet of finely mown bentgrass with splotches of Poa annua. Two metal motel chairs were over by the old man, now holing out his chips. Marlowe sat down and watched him putt, very good form with a short consistent routine. When the last ball disappeared, the old man turned and faced Marlowe, with a pained look on his gaunt and craggy face.

"Mr. Billings, please forgive the circumstances of our meeting. Roy sometimes takes my instructions too literally. Would you like some ice for your head?"

"Yeah, probably a good idea."

The workman came down the ladder, and gave Marlowe a wink on his way inside. The old man slowly walked over and sat beside Marlowe, holding an old copper Bullseye putter in his hands. He fiddled with his grip, loosening and tightening as he spoke.

"Roy forgets he's no longer up in Florence. I'm his godfather, was good friends with his banker father, who's passed on. He accidentally ran over him when Roy was two; the boy was never right after that. Before he died, he asked me to help Roy when he got out of prison. Everyone deserves a second chance—don't you think so, Mr. Billings?"

"Depends—some do and some don't. Would have preferred not running into him."

"Do you remember me, Mr. Billings? We met once many years ago."

Marlowe turned and stared at the ancient's profile.

"Can't say I do. Perhaps if you told me your name?"

"I'm Delbert Jenkins, you knocked up one of my granddaughters when she was a teenager. We met once or twice that summer—1976 I believe. She would bring you to the pool at the club."

"Candy? We went out for a while but she stopped seeing me, never told me why."

"Abortion was illegal then. I had to send her across the border to a sympathetic Mexican doctor. When she got back, I arranged for her to attend a boarding school back east."

Marlowe stared at the house feeling woozy. Roy reappeared, avoiding the green with his work boots, and handed Marlowe a bag of frozen peas. Marlowe placed it against his head and winced.

"I never knew she got pregnant. How did you find me anyway?"

"I heard you were back in town. I have friends at the DMV—they gave me your address, and Roy followed you to the park. I donated that land, by the way."

"So this is your revenge, Mr. Jenkins?"

"No, this is not about Candy—it's about her older brother."

Marlowe felt a jolt of adrenaline, oh shit.

"George?"

"Yes, I'm sure you've seen it in the papers. He was murdered and left to rot on a public golf course. You wouldn't happen to know anything about that, would you?"

Marlowe turned to look at the old man again, still staring straight ahead, a jaw muscle twitching with his pulse.

"Only what I've read—why would you think I know anything?"

"Someone involved with the investigation mentioned your name to me, Mr. Billings. I'm giving you an opportunity to explain what happened. Perhaps it was an accident, and I can help clear things up."

"I have no idea what you're talking about. What investigation? No one has spoken to me about anything."

"Oh, I imagine the authorities will soon enough; they have their own ways of doing things. Personally, I've always felt a direct approach yields the best results."

Marlowe brought the bag of peas down from his head and put it on a small ceramic table. He'd had enough.

"If you don't mind, I'd like to take my leave. Roy there could have killed me, but since I caused you grief with Candy we'll call it even. I have no idea who killed George, only that he was a spoiled shit who never grew up— maybe you had something to do with that, Mr. Jenkins?"

The old man stayed frozen. Marlowe wasn't quite sure he'd heard him. Jenkins finally turned and looked right at him.

"Do you play golf, Mr. Billings?"

"I like to chase it around, why?"

"What's your handicap?"

"About an eight, I guess."

"Do you mind if I watch you chip a few balls? I'd like to see your form. Once again, I apologize for Roy's over-exuberance. He'll be happy to give you a ride back if you would only . . ."

Marlowe stared back, but could only see a sad old man. Had dementia set in? He got up and grabbed an old Wilson Staff 9-iron resting against a tree. Pulling a pin on the green, three range balls popped out. Using the back of the club, he knocked them over to the long grass. He put a ball back in his stance, weight and hands forward to deloft the club. The first chip landed just on, rolling a few feet past the hole. The second was a little short, but the third wound up about an inch away and hole high.

Woozy again, using the club for support, Marlowe turned and looked at the old man. Brain on fire, he felt like puking, a concussion for sure.

"Well done. Roy, please take Mr. Billings back to his car."

Marlowe held the old patriarch's gaze.

"You think this is okay? Damn near kill me, ask a few questions, send me on my way with a pat on the back?"

The old man didn't react, but slowly got up and made his way to the house. Roy walked up and winked at Marlowe again, then nodded toward the van.

"No way, Jose. I'd rather walk. You and your boss are fuckin' crazy. I oughta call the cops."

The ancient paused on the green.

"I'm afraid they won't be much help to you, Mr. Billings. Roy, please call him a taxi."

CHAPTER 14

Chavez woke after dreaming of his late grandmother taking him downtown to get ice cream. The shop on Meyer no longer existed, torn down with the rest of it. In the dream, he was still a child and happy to be with abuelita. After they ordered, a bearded bum walked in, bleeding from stab wounds and asking for help. Nana got up with the napkin dispenser, started pulling them out one by one, stuffing them into the man's wounds. The bum groaned then turned to Chavez with a beatific smile—it was el Señor.

Hijole!

The dream put Chavez in a wistful mood. Dunking a stale concha into his coffee he thought about Nestor, Marlowe, Jenkins, how they all fit. He'd taken seminars where behavioral experts warned of relying on one's intuition, but Chavez didn't know any other way to run a case. He'd been wrong a few times, fooled himself really, but usually his instincts guided him in the right direction. He knew he had to interrogate Nestor or Marlowe next, pick the one most likely to crack. That wouldn't be Nestor, but he liked Marlowe and hoped he wasn't too mixed up in this *desmadre*. Honest golfers were hard to come by—people were generally full of shit, and golf really brings that out. As for Jenkins, fuck him. He was safe from prosecution for the old murder; too much time had passed and influence gained, but Chavez would never tell him that. Let him sweat it out—that is, if the living cadaver still perspired.

Chavez cleaned up and drove back out to Fred Enke to grill the staff one more time. Letting his mind wander, riffing on it all, he sang along to Cisco Kid on the radio.

Eat the salted peanuts out the can . . .

The trap raked to leave no footprints—why? Seems a bit much, unnecessary given how loose the sand was. And why not just dump George in the desert? Why a fucking golf course? He laughed to himself, goddamn crazy case!

He pulled into the course and took another look at number 10. It was the easiest hole to access from the lot—just a bit of empty desert, then the fairway. The golfer in him wondered why it wasn't number 1; had the two nines been switched around? 10 was a flat and straight par-5, no real hazards to speak of, easy to get players out in good time. Number 1 was a tight dogleg, with water on the right. That should be 10, he thought, not an easy hole at all, better to be warmed up before playing it. One of his pet peeves was hazards that only affected bad golfers, like a small pond right in front of a tee. Good players don't see the water—they pick a target and let it fly. Duffers tense up, dump a couple in the drink, ruining their round and slowing play down for everybody. It was the same in life; why put obstacles in front of people when there's no need? Why hang up a kid with a possession bust and deny him an education? Or put a landscaper out of work over a cracked windshield? Chavez hated the way poverty was criminalized, but kept his thoughts to himself around the brass. All they cared about was the city budget, keep them law-enforcement dollars flowing, maybe a dumb-ass tank for the SWAT team.

Gringos!

Catching the starter off guard, Chavez flashed his badge. He could smell the booze.

"Detective Chavez, Tucson Police Department. Your name is?"

"Call me Rudy—everyone else does."

Staring at his red, bulbous nose, Chavez didn't have to guess how he got his nickname.

"Okay, Rudolph, could I see the starter's sheet for last Sunday?"

"Very funny. This about the stiff you found?"

"Correct. I told your boss not to throw anything out."

"Oh, we have to keep them anyhow in case the city audits us. They compare the names with the green fees collected in the clubhouse. Wouldn't want anyone playing for free now, would we?"

Hearing spikes on concrete, Chavez moved aside to let a threesome check in. Looking down the 1st fairway, Chavez could see a hacker still looking for his ball, as if a duck or frog might have tossed it back in play. The threesome laughed at something Rudy said, then set off. Chavez felt a pull, wishing he could join them.

"Okay Rudy, hand it over. I know you got it right there, trying to solve the case for me."

"Ha! I have been studying it. I know the old farts who found the body, all good guys."

Chavez took the sheet and let out a breath. First off at 5:30 a.m., one Marlowe Billings.

Bingo!

"I'll be taking this as evidence. This single that started the day—his name ring a bell?"

Chavez showed him the sheet, knowing something written down has a different effect on the brain than if he'd just said the name.

"Marlowe, Marlowe Billings. Decent golfer, showed up a few months back. At first he was rusty as hell, could only play nine. Practices a lot, very polite. Not a long hitter, but breaks 80 occasionally."

"Jesus Mary, you keep profiles on all the golfers out here?"

"Nah, but I like to play on my days off. I've enjoyed a few rounds with him. Good short game. He's not involved in this, is he?"

"That's to be determined. If you see him, don't mention this conversation. I'm just at the sorting out stage. Okay, Rudy, I'll leave you to it."

"Mum's the word. Say hello to your uncle Ernie for me."

Chavez gave him a funny look.

"How'd you know that?"

"I used to work at El Rio. He was always talking proudly about his nephew. I figured how many Chavezes could be detectives?"

"True, just one Mexican—and that's me—and a black dude from Detroit."

"Larry Williams—now that guy can really launch it. He's with the men's club here."

"Larry plays? He never told me."

Rudy found his flask, took a sip, then offered it to Chavez, who waved it away.

"Golf is its own universe, Detective. It can explain all of God's mysteries one way or another, but only if you let it."

"Well, I ain't gonna argue with that. Say, are the greens mowed every morning? Traps raked?"

"Pretty much, but we're short a guy now."

"Since when?"

"Since right after your stiff was found. It's a pity, too. Paco was a hard worker."

"He got a last name?"

"He went by Ramos, but I doubt that's his real name—barely spoke English."

"Why'd he quit?"

"Just disappeared, probably back to Mexico."

"If he shows back up, call me, I want to talk to him."

"Will do, Detective—hit 'em long and straight."

Heading back to his car, Chavez took one more look at number 10. A group on the tee was getting angsty, waiting for a dreamer in the fairway hoping to get on the green in two shots. As the green cleared, he reverse pivoted and topped an ugly 3-wood, winding up where he should have hit a lay-up five minutes before.

Hackers!

Chavez drove back downtown and debated bringing Marlowe in for questioning. He didn't like where this case was going—it offended his sense of order, that someone with impeccable golf manners could be a killer. He knew that was absurd, laughed then sneezed, scaring an old woman at a red light. Another cholo classic started to play, filling his heart with joy and loss.

Never, I never met a girl like you in my life . . .

CHAPTER 15

Marlowe woke with a blazing headache. He'd lost every street fight he'd been in, so concussions were nothing new. Staring at the popcorn ceiling, he wished he could go back to sleep, but that was impossible. He made his way to the kitchen, made coffee, and leafed through an old *Arizona Highways*. It featured vivid color pictures of Oak Creek Canyon, kids having fun at Slide Rock. He'd done the same at their age, seemed like a century ago. Taking the mag with him, he sat on the john trying not to scheme. He wanted to escape, run as far away as possible. Amsterdam beckoned, score at the train station, jump off a building just like Herman Brood.

Fuck this shit.

Marlowe wiped his ass and heard the phone ring. He quickly washed his hands and answered the slimline hanging on the wall.

"About time, *ese*, you still asleep?"

"Can't a man shit in peace? What do you want?"

"Dude, don't be like that—ain't we friends?"

"Go on."

"I need your help with something—meet me down at the Chicago Store around noon. You remember old Joe, no?"

"How could I forget? What kind of help, Nestor?"

"No seas un culero guero, don't make me come looking for your white ass."

The line went dead, Marlowe listened to the concert A dial tone. He thought about calling the cops, just shut this shit down. He didn't owe Nestor anything—the opposite, in fact. Not to mention old man Jenkins, fucker was crazy and nearly killed him. Why was this happening to him? All he wanted was to kick his habit and get La Española back. If going to rehab was the right move, why was everything flying out of control?

Looking at the clock, he decided to hit a meeting first, settle his mind. He hung up and recited the serenity prayer, but choked on the last of it. *Wisdom to know the difference*, yeah right.

Nervous after drinking too much shitty coffee, Marlowe left the meeting early to a few judgmental stares. He found Nestor upstairs at the Chicago Store, knee deep in Mosrite guitars. The iconic Tucson store was a cavernous three-story affair of red brick, with sidewalk plate-glass windows, the scene of Marlowe's felony.

"Well looky here, homie. You made it."

"Against my better judgment."

Nestor held up a candy-apple–red beauty.

"Whaddya think? Just like Johnny Ramone."

"On your wall sure, but they don't stay in tune."

"I'm supposed to pick up something sweet for a friend of mine—she likes to play."

"You need me for this?"

"Not really, but I thought we could continue our conversation. You know, about finding Georgie boy, qué raro güero."

"Strange? That's one word for it, let me see it."

Marlowe took the guitar and looked it over. Straight neck, bridge solid with the Bigsby whammy. He tuned it up and twanged a little.

"What if I just go to the cops, tell 'em what I know, let them figure it out."

He started on a chunky riff, singing along.

"I don't care about that girl, I don't care about this world, I don't care."

"Oh, you won't do that, amigo."

Marlowe stopped in the middle of the chorus.

"Why not? You're fuckin' with me bigtime, Nestor. I don't need this shit."

"You fuckin' white boys just don't get it. It was fate, destiny brought us back together."

Marlowe stopped playing and stared at Nestor, who returned the look with pinned eyes.

"Or maybe I OD'ed back in Spain, and this is purgatory. None of it makes sense—nada."

"So whaddya think?"

"You know what I think—I don't want any part of this. Whatever it is, I don't wanna know."

"No, the guitar, *ese*—should I buy it?"

They looked around a little more upstairs and down, vintage musical gear strewn about like a tornado hit. Minimoogs, Echoplexes, Baldwin amps, Airline guitars, a treasure trove of weirdness mixed in with more prosaic Gibson and Fender gear. It looked like chaos, but good deals were rare. Joe knew the true worth of almost every item. How he collected so much coolness no one knew, but it all wound up here in downtown Tucson. Eyes full, they headed for the cashier to pay for the guitar, and it was Joe himself manning the register.

"So you found yourselves a prize, did you? That there is a good guitar."

Nestor looked at Marlowe to handle the negotiation.

"It's a piece of junk, Joe, you know that. We need it for a prop in a play."

"A plaaaay? What's this play about, gentlemen? Say, you look familiar—you famous?"

"It's about a surf band, Joe—they wind up on Mars. What difference does it make?"

"Wait I know, you're that punk rocker who busted my window, made me come down here in my pajamas—that wasn't nice."

Nestor laughed.

"Well, I paid the restitution, or my girlfriend did. Misspent youth and all that. How much, Joe?"

"A thousand dollars, cash. We can finance for another hundred or so."

Marlowe put the guitar down on the counter.

"Let's go, Nestor. Joe's lost his mind today."

"Lost my mind? Lost my mind? That there is a classic instrument, very hot pick-ups. The Ventures model, worth twice what I asked."

"Joe, it's crap, no one cares about The Ventures anymore. We just like the finish—we'll give you two hundred dollars."

"Two hundred?! You break my window, ruin my night, come back a decade later and insult me with that offer?"

"It doesn't even work, we plugged it in and just got space buzz."

"Well, take it downstairs to Rainer—he'll fix it. Let me get him right now."

"Don't bother Rainer—okay, three hundred bucks."

"Four!"

Marlowe looked at Nestor, who gave him a nod.

"Okay, four hundred, but find a case for it, and not flimsy cardboard, deal?"

"Mark, find a case for this Mosrite here, let's see the green before I change my mind."

Marlowe walked out with Nestor and the guitar, imagining he was young again. Music had been good to him, but he never felt like he belonged. He disliked most musicians, maybe because he was just a lazy writer and songs came easy. Would he ever play again? He just didn't know.

"Okay, pues, thanks for the help. This is me right here."

They stopped by a trashy champagne Cutlass Supreme, parked right in front.

"Where's the truck? This isn't your style."

"Belongs to a friend, let's put it in the trunk."

Nestor fished for his keys, then popped it open.

Marlowe swung the case up but stopped halfway, tweaking his shoulder. Below was a terrified soul, bound and gagged, eyes darting back and forth. Marlowe handed Nestor the guitar and backed away.

"What the fuck, dude? Jesus fucking Christ!"

Nestor calmly put the guitar in the trunk and shut it.

"You should thank me well—that's Paco, the dude who watched you find poor George."

Marlowe's head started to spin; he whispered in fear.

"I thought he worked for you—where are you taking him?"

"He's going back to his owner, unless he changes his mind and plays ball. Don't worry, Marlowe, you can pretend you never saw him when you call the cops."

Marlowe tried to spit, but his mouth was bone-dry. Nestor gave him a jovial pat on the back, then got in the beater and turned it over. Easing into traffic, the Olds purred like a street rod, all the money was under the hood. Marlowe stumbled toward the Montego, parked a half-block west. Passing the huge plate-glass window of his youth, he saw his reflection, then a vaguely familiar face on the other side staring right at him. Marlowe hesitated, and the man turned away and browsed through sheet music. Getting in his car, it suddenly dawned—it was the dude he'd played golf with a few days before.

Small fucking town.

CHAPTER 16

Chavez walked east to Hotel Congress, and tried to figure Marlowe out. Were these guys just amigos, him and Nestor? He'd tailed Marlowe to the same recovery meeting as before, then downtown to the Chicago Store. How could anyone legit be friends with Nestor? He watched them buy a guitar, then got the license plate of the Oldsmobile Nestor was driving. Something weird about their goodbyes—what was that about? He should bring Marlowe in for questioning, had plenty of probable cause, but something was holding him back. He made a note to pray to St. Jude, the patron saint of criminals and prisoners, but also popular with cops. A little divine intervention would be welcome; it wouldn't be the first time. Abuelita's voice came to him again, soothing in its certainty.

Fe y paciencia, mijo, faith and patience.

He entered the swamp-cooled lobby of the hotel, grateful for the temporary relief from the heat and stress. He liked to eat lunch at The Cup every month or so, see what the kids were up to. They were all pierced and tatted now, but much more mixed racially and sexually than his generation. He found them exotic and oddly sweet. They tried to look tough, but it was all an act.

Chavez ordered a topopo salad and iced tea, and imagined the hotel in John Dillinger's time. Legend had him hiding out on the third floor, before setting a fire to make his escape. Now it was a trendy hotel, restored after a few decades of flophouse degradation. He thought about *La Calle*, the square mile or so of Mexican downtown torn down for Jenkins' "civic progress." What sort of renewal would be happening now, if only given the chance? His tea tasted bitter as he mused, and he suddenly felt angry at the hipsters and yuppies enjoying lunch at the other tables. What did Carmen say about it? You can't erase the past—it only smears like mascara after a good cry.

Chavez paid his bill and headed out, nodding at the desk clerk, a tall ginger-haired Okie with a face chiseled out of stone. He'd heard him play once, fronting a band called The Cattle. He sang in a monotone wail, but played jagged, mean guitar. Chavez thought of Jenkins, same tribe really—they could be related. The old man was still dangerous, an ancient rattler with plenty of venom left. Chavez didn't want to get bit, but he wasn't gonna avoid a confrontation either. The badge was a great equalizer—that was the thing he liked best about being a cop. Maybe he liked it too much, as Carmen pointed out more than once. A '70s pop tune followed him out the door, making him sigh.

Every dream in her heart was gone
There's gonna be a showdown . . .

CHAPTER 17

Marlowe considered another recovery meeting, but chanced on finding Grum. He was still reeling from Nestor's surprise, and needed a real friend to talk it out. Grum lived behind the Boondocks, in an adobe lunger shack on a street much too wide for the traffic. This was part of Tucson's insanity, the lack of density in a desert environment. Marlowe could see it all just being abandoned once the price of water and electricity shot up to their true unsubsidized cost.

Grum answered the door half asleep, but waved Marlowe in with a grin. The living room was shambolic, but not disgusting. Marlowe found a place on the couch and closed his eyes.

"Well, well, what a nice surprise—you want some sody?"

"No thanks, Grum, rots your teeth. Sorry to bug ya, I'm not feeling so hot."

"What's the matter? Tucson got you down? Miss your woman back across the pond?"

"Nestor's got me on the hook for something I know nothing about."

"How's that? Why are you hanging with him anyway?"

"What do you mean, *hanging*?"

"Rainer called, said you two bought a guitar today. Was disappointed you didn't say hello."

"I didn't want to bug him. Nestor would only hustle him for a favor."

The bedroom door creaked open. A chunky Latina came out wearing one of Grum's dress shirts. She poured herself some Mountain Dew, grabbed a

Marlboro out of the pack on the coffee table, and went back into the cave. Marlowe gave Grum a look.

"That's Lydia, bartends at the Boondocks, sleeps here if she gets too loaded after her shift."

"Nice arrangement."

"Why don't you lay it out for me, buddy? Tell me what's really going on. I ain't a shrink, but maybe I can point you in the right direction."

"I'm the one who found George Jenkins."

"Don't bullshit me, duden, just spill it."

"I was first out at Enke and found him in a sand trap. I kept playing, didn't want to deal with the cops. Nestor had a plant out there watching, the guy fingered me. Now that dude is in Nestor's trunk, probably headed to the graveyard."

Grum cocked his head at Marlowe like a perplexed dog.

"Nestor won't tell me what he wants. Just keeps reminding me I'm an accessory after the fact."

Grum lit a cigarette and let it all sink in.

"You think he killed George?"

"No idea."

"Well, my man says there's trouble in Nogales, the plaza is up for grabs. George got in too deep is the word, way above his pay grade. Is that it, Marlowe? There has to be more."

"Old man Jenkins snatched me the other day right off the street. Wanted to know what I knew about his grandson. Said the cops have me as a suspect."

The room grew quiet as Grum smoked and pondered. Marlowe could hear a dog barking nearby, and Lydia watching *The Price Is Right* on TV.

"It's that silly goddamn game, Marlowe. Golf fucked you right in the ass."

They both cracked up, laughing like little kids. Lydia stuck her head out, shrugged, and went back to her show.

"What am I gonna do, Grum? I'm barely staying clean, and this shit's happening. I miss my wife so fuckin' much, can barely stand it. I just wanna . . ."

"Kill yourself? Why do that if it turns out to be much ado about nothing?"

"Then what, dude? Just wait to be arrested, or whacked by whoever Nestor is working for? My nerves can't take it."

"Do what you've always done—never failed before."

"And what's that?"

Grum got up and put a record on, adjusting the volume down to a nice background level.

"Split town. Go back to Spain and win her back. Stay away until this shit blows over."

"You think it will?"

"Ashes to ashes funk to funky . . ."

Marlowe picked up the melody.

"We know Major Tom's a junkie . . ."

Then both together.

"Strung out in heaven's high, hitting an all-time low!"

Fully dressed now in her own clothes, Lydia came out, rolled her eyes at the two warbling white boys, and left without a word.

CHAPTER 18

B ack at his desk, Chavez ran the Oldsmobile's plate, but it didn't match—switched out. He swore at himself for not following Nestor, but didn't want to tip him off. He thought of Marlowe's face through the window—had he made him? At an impasse, he flipped a coin that bounced off his palm and skittered across the room. The phone rang as he cursed.

"Detective Chavez."

"Hello, hello, are you in charge of the Jenkins case?"

The voice was scratchy, either from a cold or something placed over the microphone.

"Yes, I am. Who am I speaking to?"

"A friend of George Jenkins—I want to help. They shouldn't have killed him like that."

"Well, why don't you come down to the office and we'll talk about it?"

"I can't do that. My wife doesn't know I'm still friends with George—or *was* still friends. She doesn't know I still get high."

"Withholding evidence is a crime—you know that, right?"

"That's why I'm calling. You ever hear of Rancho Maravilloso? On the other side of the Rincons?"

"Yeah, sure, sold to some developers last year. Why?"

"George was a silent partner, or at least he said he was. Some very interesting people are involved the county doesn't know about. If the press caught wind, it would cause an uproar, way more than the environmental issues."

"Look, why don't we meet somewhere, you can tell me all about it."

"I've said enough. Good luck, Detective. I would be very careful—there are people in this town who are not what they seem. Goodbye."

Chavez hung up and leaned back in his wooden chair, hands behind his head. He always made fun of detective novels, but this case would make a doozy. All it was missing was a femme fatale. He thought of Carmen and felt a wince. How long had it been? They had a good thing going, until she called him *una Malinche*—that hurt. Both too proud, neither would make the first call to patch things up. He heard *abuela's* laughter, *tercos como mulas*, stubborn as mules!

He really needed to get laid.

Instead, he decided to hit some balls at El Rio, settle his nerves. Maybe work on his grip, weaken it a bit to gain more control. On the way out, he saw the quarter, stuck in a tile crack like a wheel, neither heads nor tails. Reaching down, he put it in his pocket, right next to Marlowe Billings' golf ball.

CHAPTER 19

Marlowe put a bucket under the range-ball machine and fed it a few dollar bills. He found the cacophony of the balls tumbling down pleasant, like a herd of buffalo. He'd brought only three clubs: pitching wedge, 6-iron, driver. He would start with the shortest, then work his way to the driver, before ending the session by mixing it up. He knew he should be at a meeting, but it was hard to hang with folks he'd never want a beer with. Principles before personalities was the saying, but he wasn't a thumper—just a junkie tired of being strung out.

The range at El Rio had maybe twenty stations and was a quarter full. Marlowe headed to the last place on the right, where he could practice with his back to the hackers. Unfortunately, someone was occupying that spot. As Marlowe approached, he admired the dude's swing, just a tad closed at the top, but pretty solid nonetheless.

Putting his bucket down on the adjacent tee, Marlowe stretched with his wedge behind his back, looped through his arms. He wanted to work on his take-away, keeping his right side firm, not swaying off the ball. He'd always had a nice right-to-left weight transfer, similar to throwing a ball or a punch, but knew if he wanted more consistency he had to shorten his swing. The reverse C he'd been taught as a kid was long out of fashion—it looked pretty but was much too loosey-goosey. Maybe if he tightened things up, he'd get a crisper release, producing more control and distance—wouldn't that be nice?

He knocked a half-dozen balls out of the bucket with his wedge, then started with a few quarter shots with his feet together. He tried to swing at half-speed, working on both rhythm and form. Like life, golf was about learning how to practice to get better, a process in itself. *Feel ain't real*, golf pros and shrinks tell their clients, but few actually listen.

Methodically keeping at it till the bucket was half empty, Marlowe sat down on a bench to take a break. To his left he watched a few obscene swings, but the guy on his right was launching some impressive drives, smacking them into the net 250 yards out. Something about his swing rang a bell—he'd seen it before.

"Chavez, is that you? You're scaring those guys on 17."

Chavez turned and looked at Marlowe, giving him a strange look.

"We played a few days ago at Randolph, you dropped out after nine leaving me with that fatty, remember?"

"Yeah, sure—how ya doing? Marvin, right?"

"Marlowe's my name. Funny seeing you here. I swore I saw you at The Chicago Store—was that you?"

"Yeah, I was picking up some sheet music for my niece—she loves Elton John."

"Pretty weird, no? Like we're following each other."

"It's a small town."

"True, but it keeps growing like a cancer. So how's it going—you figure this crazy game out yet?"

Chavez sat down and swiveled to face Marlowe.

"I don't play enough to get much better. I practice twice a week, so I feel somewhat comfortable on the course. Just don't have the time."

"Tied to a desk I imagine. Yeah, that makes it tough."

"Not exactly chained inside, but I have to keep weird hours. How do *you* manage?"

"Shit, I'm a musician, bunch of us are golf junkies. When I lived in L.A. saw quite a few actors on the links, too. Show biz is feast or famine, with lots of downtime, so why not play?"

Chavez looked at Marlowe like he was deciding something.

"Well, I'm a cop. This is cheaper than therapy and twice the fun."

"A cop? You must be a detective then—what division?"

"Homicide."

Marlowe grew quiet. What were the odds? He knew Chavez couldn't possibly be following him, but still it made him nervous. Chavez grinned.

"See, that's why I generally don't tell anyone what I do. I bet priests have the same problem, lawyers maybe."

"Nah, I have no problem with the police. Got into trouble as a kid, but that was enough."

"You wouldn't be the first. After twenty, most everyone mellows out. Way too many people in prison for stupid shit they did as teenagers."

"Yeah, I know a few. Look, you got a card or something? Maybe we can get a regular game going. It was nice playing with a good golfer for once. I'm flexible so give me a day's notice and I'll be there."

"Yeah, why not? I hope you ain't hustling me—we cops are suspicious."

"Wish I was good enough to hustle—you ever hear of Titanic Thompson?"

"Oh sure, read plenty, but my favorite was Trevino beating some country-club pro using only a Dr. Pepper bottle and a shovel."

"Trevino was awesome, that strange swing where he pushes it out right. Never hit a hook—brilliant. They say Ray Floyd handed him his shoes once to polish, thought he was the locker room attendant. Trevino didn't say a word, then met him on the first tee for their match. Imagine Ray's surprise."

Laughing, they both went back to their practice. After hitting the last ball, Chavez gave a little whistle and handed Marlowe his card.

"Call me anytime. I never know when I can sneak out for at least nine."

"Thanks, Detective. Maybe the golf gods are making us cross paths like this, wouldn't want to piss 'em off."

"No indeed. You take it easy, Marlowe—keep it in the short grass."

Driving home, Marlowe thought of Chavez and whether he should spill his guts. He could see dark cumulus clouds forming to the south, a late-season chubasco. The radio warned of flash floods, then played an old Mark Lindsay chestnut, making Marlowe smile.

Arizona, take off your hobo shoes
Arizona, hey won't you go my way?

Back Nine

CHAPTER 20

Don Luis watched the terrain get more and more desolate. Flying north from Durango in a Cessna T-41 Mescalero, it was just him and the pilot. The back two seats were removed years ago, but no contraband was onboard. He took it all in, the vast Chihuahuan Desert with just a forlorn cow here and there. It was easy to fathom the north of Mexico as its frontier, something most gringos never understood. It was still Mexico's wild west, with the Yaquis her Apaches, marginalized but never conquered. They were reliable contrabandistas, with family relationships on both sides of the border keeping things stable, until recently that is. Don Luis was on a mission, sent by his banker boss in Polanco to straighten out the Nogales plaza, under siege by forces unknown. Don Luis believed it was the Colombians, using the Sinaloans as proxies, trying to get the cost of transport down for their beloved cocaine. He hated the drug, but it was more popular than sex, and the profits unbelievable. If people wanted to ruin their lives, he was happy to oblige—he didn't create the demand.

Pinche Pericos!

Like Zapata, Don Luis took shit from no one, regardless of class. He got his first job sweeping courts at a tennis resort, moonlighting as a lookout *halcón* for a local gang. He climbed the ranks by not talking shit, and taking responsibility when things went bad. Soon he had his own business in Cuernavaca, a city full of rich divorcees from Mexico City and their bratty kids, all looking to get high. After running a few loads to the border, then, doing some favors for an influential político, he found himself with a new jefe in Polanco. He took out an uncooperative judge in Puebla, becoming *Don* Luis overnight. He took no pleasure in the killing, but business was business, and it was greed that really did the guy in. Now here he was, flying high above his beloved Mexico, but feeling cautious, like a coyote sniffing around a baited trap.

He didn't like el norte, which was basically everything north of Durango. They were gringoized—*pochos*, all of them. The cliche *poor Mexico, so far from God and so close to the United States* was true enough, but forgives Spain all her transgressions against la patria. Don Luis *was* patriotic, but not delusional. He understood the basic unfairness of Mexico, rooted in racist and classist beliefs, while deifying Montezuma. Still, the United States was worse, despite all the Hollywood propaganda. He knew to be careful with this Jenkins guy, to not use Mexican logic to predict his behavior. That could get him killed—he'd seen it time and again.

They landed on a rancher's private strip, just south of Nogales. Don Luis hopped into a waiting Ford Bronco and chuckled at the absurdity of a kid from Morelos up here in Pancho Villa land. Pancho was a ruffian, a *payaso*, and not worth the lead he was shot full of. Zapata, on the other hand, was the real deal, an actual revolutionary figure. Although he'd barely attended school, Don Luis liked to read histories of Mexico, especially by Enrique Krauze. The grand político Hank González, aka *El Profesor*, was another hero, who famously said a politician who is poor is a poor politician.

Pinche cabrón!

Finally making it to the Fray Marcos Hotel, Don Luis took a shower and planned his strategy. He wished he could handle this on the Mexican side, but knew he had to cross the border. Polanco warned that Jenkins would not enter Sonora, and knew the Mexican mind well, having grown up in a Tucson barrio. With the death of his grandson, the old man undoubtedly wanted *venganza*, but whether he could be accommodated without upsetting the balance between Polanco and Sinaloa was the question.

Don Luis mused on it all, drinking tequila he found in the mini-bar. Gringos always wanted complete control, as if that was possible, but Mexican fatalism also had its limits. To be overly ambitious was looked down upon in Mexico, whereas to have little was a sin in the United States. Don Luis understood both points of view; life was a balancing act, with borders everywhere. The future might be certain, but how one arrives there is always a mystery.

CHAPTER 21

havez slept in late, then felt guilty and decided on some surveillance. He sipped his second coffee while parked down the street from the Goat Lady's house, watching who was coming in and out. He figured Nestor was probably strung out, and she had the best dope in town. It had been over a week now since George Jenkins was found, and Chavez's lieutenant raised an eyebrow every time he saw him. He didn't even want to think about the pressure coming from Jenkins, the old ghoul pulling strings from Tucson to D.C.

Normally on a Sunday, Chavez would be knocking it around at El Rio, just a few streets over. But Sunday was a good junkie day, too, with the trade starting late morning. The Goat Lady was super cagey, never really caught a major case. Her moniker came from Mexican slang for heroin: *chiva*. Seldom keeping much weight at the house, the old wrinkled *abuela* always befuddled the judge whenever she got busted. She would claim she didn't know how the dope got there, that she had nephews, cousins, and grandkids constantly coming and going. How was she to know what they were up to?

Pretty slick.

After two hours and a few buyers, Chavez turned the key in the ignition to go eat some pozole at Tanias. Halfway down the block, he passed the beat-up Oldsmobile Nestor had been driving the other day. Flipping a U-turn, he watched as it pulled up to the Goat Lady's place. Nestor wasn't driving; it was a guy dressed in the working khaki uniform of groundskeepers and landscapers everywhere.

Chavez watched the man open the trunk and grab some shopping bags from Food City. He entered the house without knocking—had to be family. Stomach rumbling, Chavez hoped this wouldn't be a long visit and the pozole wouldn't sell out before he got there. Thankfully, the dude came out ten minutes later, and Chavez followed him down the street, lighting him up as they approached Speedway. Maybe it was hunger, but Chavez realized he fucked up when the guy ignored his lights and took off like a jackrabbit. Now what? Chase him solo against regulation, or call in for backup?

Fuck it. Tanias.

Adding fresh radish, cilantro, onion, cabbage, crushed red pepper, and lime, Chavez slurped the pork stew and thought about the case. Nestor was suspect number one, for sure, but seeing Marlowe's face when Nestor opened the Olds' trunk intrigued him. It was like he'd seen a ghost—or that scene from *Repo Man*. His hunch about the Goat Lady proved correct, but what was really going on? He knew there was trouble in Sonora, a well-built tunnel had recently been uncovered in Nogales, someone must have ratted. Still, the Goat Lady's connections went back generations, her Yaqui family ties unbreakable. This was the trouble with even routine drug murders—the bigger story was rarely simple. The higher one went, the more complicated it got, with the DEA often shielding major suspects. The way George was placed in the bunker—was that a warning? At the same time, there was no sign of torture, just a bashed-in skull, pretty respectful actually.

Leaving a tenner on the table, Chavez nodded to a few familiar faces on his way out, then decided to head to El Rio to stroke some putts. Driving north on Grande he passed Pat's Chili Dogs, and there was the Olds, parked right out front.

No fucking way.

Pulling in next to the Cutlass, he got out with gun drawn, and opened the passenger side door. The driver was eating a chili dog while holding a Coke. Chavez pointed his gun at him as he slid into the passenger seat.

"Sorry to disturb your lunch. I'm Detective Chavez, and I have some questions for you."

"I know you find me. Sorry no stop. I come here to eat before la cárcel."

Chavez knew right away the man was a Mexican national, but decided to pretend he couldn't speak Spanish very well.

"You have a gun in the car?"

Like a lot of people learning a second language, the guy understood more than he could speak, and shook his head no.

"Put that dog down and keep your hands on the wheel. What's your name?"

"Paco. I no want trouble, just take me to la cárcel."

Chavez chuckled.

"You're in quite a hurry to be locked up, how come?"

"No quiero ningún problema."

"How do you know the Goat Lady?"

"She my . . . how you say? *Ella es mi tía abuela.*"

"Your *tía abuela*? Oh, your aunt—your great-aunt. What were you delivering to her?"

"*Las provisiones*, I bring every Sunday."

"No *heroína*?"

"*Dios mio no. No soy un traficante.*"

"*Y su tía?*"

"*She mi familia.*"

Chavez sighed, put his gun away, and took a sip of Paco's Coke.

"Where do you work?"

"*En un campo de golf.*"

"Yeah? Which one?"

"Fred Enke."

Chavez's body started to tingle.

"Cómo conoces a Nestor?"

"He help me. *Pagó mi factura."*

"Paid your bill? From the border? La frontera? You owed money to a *pollero?"*

"Sí."

Chavez's cell phone rang, startling him. He'd only had one for a few months, hated it, and mostly kept it on mute. Fumbling, he managed to answer on the fourth ring.

"Chavez here. Hey, Marlowe, how ya doing? Sure, would love to sneak out. What about Fred Enke? Uh, let me see, how 'bout in an hour or so? Okay, see ya then."

Chavez felt high, like he'd ripped a huge bong hit back in his cousin's bedroom.

"Muy bien, Paco, we're gonna take a little ride, but finish your chili dog first—hell, I might have one, too."

"La cárcel?"

"Fuck no, el campo de golf."

CHAPTER 22

Marlowe hadn't been back to Fred Enke since finding George Jenkins, but figured why not spill his guts to Chavez where it all started? Driving south on Kolb, he felt light as a feather, the monkey on his back if not removed, then safely in a cage where he could poke it with a stick. Calling Chavez was the next right move, something his folksy counselor often talked about in rehab. You can't rebuild your life in a day, only brick by brick. Golf was the same: one shot at a time.

He arrived at the course, happy to find the parking lot half-empty—there would be no trouble getting out to play. He put on his spikes, reviewed the track, and decided to leave his driver behind since the course was so tight. Why bring a club you'd only use once or twice? Better to just groove a 3- or 5-wood all day long. Yeah, baby.

Enjoying the familiar steel-cleat-to-asphalt crunch, Marlowe glanced at number 10's tee box and swore it was the same group of codgers from the day he found the corpse. He hoped he'd still be playing at their age, having fun knocking it around with your buds. He thought about their wives, grateful for a few hours of relief from their husbands. They might complain about all the golf they played, but it was all an act.

Marlowe headed to the putting green below the clubhouse. Uncertain when Chavez would arrive, he didn't bother to leave their names with the starter. He was just getting ready to grab a drink when he saw Chavez coming down the path with another guy carrying his clubs. Marlowe raised a brow, and Chavez explained.

"I brought a caddie—he'll carry both our bags if you want. Tell the starter we're ready, I'll pick up the green fees inside. You can pay me later."

Marlowe gave the caddie a closer look and nearly shat his pants. What the fuck? They eyed each other warily as Chavez went inside.

"So you made it out of that trunk alive, and here you are with a cop."

"No quiero ningún problema, estamos chingados."

"Yes, indeed, we are truly fucked. Did you really see me find that body like Nestor said?"

"Yes, I see el lagartijo, then you."

"Did you rake the trap?"

"Lo siento, no entiendo."

Marlowe shrugged, fuck it, might as well get it over with. He felt depleted, no hustle left. He grabbed his bag and headed for the starter. It was the same crusty dude as always; he'd played a couple rounds with him a few months before.

"Hey, Rudy—how's tricks? I got a twosome going out."

"What about Paco there? He needs his own sticks."

"Gonna caddie."

"Caddie? This ain't Tucson Country Club. Well, okay, I saw he came with the Detective, but slip me a fiver if you got it."

Marlowe looked through his wallet, but could only find a ten dollar bill, nothing smaller.

Rudy smiled while taking a nip from his flask.

"Oh, that's even better. Hit 'em sweet and watch for snakes—I've gotten a few reports."

Marlowe walked downhill to the first tee, careful not to slip on the concrete in his spikes. He took out his 5-wood and warmed up with some stretches. Chavez soon joined him, with Paco right behind.

"So what's the deal? He under arrest or something? Working off his sentence?"

"Nah, this is Paco. Paco este es Marlowe—you've never met before, right?"

Paco looked at Marlowe and nodded.

"Paco's English ain't too good, but he's a greenskeeper here and knows the course. Ain't that right, Paco?"

Paco grimaced.

"Ya no trabajo aquí."

Chavez laughed.

"Read my putts well and maybe I can get your old job back."

Marlowe flipped a tee and got the honor. He marked his ball in the usual fashion, teed it up, and cut a little fade hugging the left side, leaving about a 7-iron in. Chavez took out his driver and cut the dogleg, a beautiful drive but risky as hell. Marlowe looked at him funny.

"I feel lucky today, Marlowe. No guts, no glory."

They grinned at each other and started the round. Paco motioned he could carry both bags, but Marlowe waved him off.

"No caddie for me, Paco, gracias. I do a fine job myself."

"You good golfer?"

Marlowe muttered to himself . . .

"When I'm not being framed for murder, yeah. Today we'll see."

Closer than he thought, Marlowe knocked an 8-iron to the middle of the green. Chavez's drive had taken a weird bounce, but he found his ball on the cart path and elected to not take a drop. He bumped a chip into the hill, where it tumbled up and onto the putting surface, winding up 6 feet short of the pin. Marlowe whistled in appreciation.

"Sweet shot that, well done."

"That's an El Rio special, all those old-school turtleback greens."

Marlowe two-putted for par, but Chavez came up a few inches short for birdie. Paco, with pin in hand, reached down to grab Chavez's ball, but

Chavez waved him off and putted out, then chided himself like good golfers do.

"Never up, never in, just like with the missus—if I had one that is. You married, Marlowe?"

"I guess so—she's back in Spain, currently separated."

"Sorry to hear that."

They headed for the next tee, pleased to have avoided a big number on a dangerous opening hole. So many rounds are ruined early, just like life. The rest of the nine flowed smoothly, like a nice Monday that turns into a beautiful week. Both players kept mostly to themselves, with Paco giving advice when asked. Making the turn, Chavez excused himself to take a whiz in the clubhouse. Marlowe waited on 10 with Paco, and finally broke the ice.

"Where were you when I found George?"

"En mi carro."

"Dónde?"

Paco pointed to the far end of the parking lot, right by the entrance and next to the 10th green.

"Who killed him?"

"No sé, tal vez murió en accidente."

"Yeah sure, Nestor?"

"Quién sabe? Ask tu amigo."

"Did you rake the trap?"

Before Paco could answer, Chavez appeared, apologizing for the delay. Having the honor after a birdie on 8, he nailed his driver right down the middle, putting eagle into play. Marlowe, feeling anxious, pushed his 3-wood right, winding up pretty much where he'd been last time out. He played the next two shots prudently, and left his approach pin-high to a center-left hole position. Chavez went for it in two and came up short, but in good position to make birdie.

Walking up to the green, it all came flooding back: the Gila monster, George's frozen eyes, the curious wasp. Marlowe shivered in the heat—was it all just a fever dream? Maybe he'd overdosed back in Spain, and this was purgatory? He thought of *Jacob's Ladder*—he'd seen it just off the Puerta Del Sol after scoring from the gypsy. Nodding out in the theater, he watched it twice. Later that night, half asleep, he felt a darkness seeping under the bedroom door, engulfing him. He tried to scream, but no sound came out. He ran into the kitchen, where La Española was cleaning up. He came up to her from behind, wanting a hug, but she turned around, saw his pinned eyes and pushed him away in disgust.

Loser!

Breathing slow to calm himself, Marlowe decided to confess to everything after the round. Chavez took out his putter, then smacked a Texas wedge through the green and into the back right sand trap. Marlowe looked at him funny, but Chavez wouldn't meet his gaze. What the fuck? Marlowe grabbed his own putter, and waited for Chavez to play his bunker shot while Paco found a rake.

"Hey come here for a sec, I got a funny lie."

Marlowe walked over and joined Chavez peering down above the trap.

"This is where you found him—must have been a shock."

Marlowe felt a punch to the belly, his mouth dry as dirt.

"Paco, you watched the whole thing, verdad?"

Paco looked up from below, shrugging his shoulders in fatalistic agreement.

Marlowe rasped . . .

"His eyes were open, there was a wasp, it went into his mouth and he didn't move—that's how I knew he was dead."

"Why didn't you go back to the clubhouse, call the police?"

"I don't know why—I just didn't. I figured someone else would find him soon enough."

They heard a whistle and a shout from behind. Looking back, a foursome was in the fairway waiting to hit their approach shots. Marlowe stared at Chavez, who gave the group a dirty look.

"Paco, did you dump the body here? Dime la verdad!"

"No jefe!"

"What are you gonna do, Detective?"

"Paco, grab my ball and rake the trap, let's all take par here and move on—sound fair, Mr. Billings?"

Marlowe shook his head in disbelief. He picked up his bag, which now felt light as air. A huge weight lifted from his chest, a pressure building since his last hit of heroin. On the next tee, a squadron of javelina trotted across the fairway, the babies' fur a reddish hue. Marlowe watched in wonder, witnesses to his confession.

Outside of the usual golf etiquette, Chavez remained silent the rest of their match. They both shot 80, but tainted by the gentlemen's agreement on 10. After shaking hands, Marlowe forked over a Jackson for his green fee, which Chavez accepted without a word. They walked together to their cars, the post-round glow in effect.

"Okay, Marlowe, I don't have to tell you to stick around. I know you're involved in this murder, at least peripherally, but I don't think you killed him."

"It's just bad luck, a coincidence."

"Nestor García is no coincidence. I would be very careful if I was you."

"I'm more worried about old man Jenkins—fucker's goon nearly killed me."

Chavez stopped and looked at him funny.

"Roy? I'm too hungry and tired to follow that up. Meet me tomorrow for breakfast at Robert's at Grant and Country Club, say 9 o'clock?"

"Sure, love their pies."

"You can buy me breakfast, I would've birdied 10 no problem, goddamn work always finds a way to fuck up a round. C'mon, Paco, let's get us another Pat's chili dog—you're gonna tell me all you know about this crazy fucking case."

"No voy a la cárcel?"

"No jail today, Paco. I just hope you don't wind up like George Jenkins."

"Me too, jefe, ojalá!"

CHAPTER 23

D on Luis woke up full of nostalgia. His first trip to the border had been for a narco who owned paint and body shops in Phoenix. Only fifteen, Don Luis got paid five thousand dollars to drive a load of weed from Morelos to Agua Prieta. When he gave half the money to his mother, she cried and told him he would get killed one day, but his siblings were hungry and God knew what was right. After that, he only used Western Union to send her money, and joined the Cuernavaca tennis club as a full member. He loved to play; it was an honest game that required skill and strategy, especially doubles. Fútbol was Mexico's obsession, but tennis was his own, a secret he kept mostly to himself.

After breakfast, he got in line to cross the border just a few blocks away. The kid who drove him from the ranch waited with him, then disappeared as Don Luis entered the U.S. Customs and Border Patrol building. He carried no luggage, blending in with the maquiladora traffic. He showed a border crossing card, answered a few questions, and was let through. Walking past van services to Tucson and Phoenix, he made his way to a paid parking lot, where a short young woman dressed in white linen pants and a China Poblana blouse was waiting next to a late-model white Suburban.

"Don Luis? Me llamo Juanita. Have you had a nice journey?"

"Hola, Juanita. Yes, tu tío dice que eres muy capaz."

Don Luis felt a pang of regret; she didn't know her uncle would soon be killed for hiding money in Miami.

"No te fallaré, Don Luis, es un placer. Less scrutiny, uh, menos escrutinio con una mujer."

"Absolutamente, actúes como mi hija, vamanos!"

Telling Juanita to take the long way, they got off of I-19 and were soon in beautiful ranch country leading to Patagonia. This was all Spanish territory at one time, he told her, with land grants flowing through to Mexican independence until the Treaty of La Mesilla. Juanita looked at him funny and commented in English.

"You mean the Gadsden Purchase?"

Don Luis sighed—what's the use? The gringos had stolen more than just land; they took Mexican culture away from her people, replacing it with the cold hard ways of Protestant life. Now *los evangélicos* were everywhere, eroding the syncretic Catholicism that held Mexico together. It was one of the reasons he refused to improve his English, perhaps too prideful given the business he was in, but fuck gringos and their Disneyland.

Stopping in Patagonia to take a piss, Don Luis didn't see any Mexicans anywhere, although they were only a few miles from the border. He bought some beef jerky from the local market, asking to use the toilet. The clerk pointed to the rear, then spoke to his back.

"Can't you read English?"

He turned around and gave her a look.

"Me dijiste algo?"

She looked down, pretending to be busy. This was something Don Luis never understood, the abject rudeness of the United States. Racism he could accept—hell, Mexico had plenty of that, but to be impolite for no reason made him angry. On the bathroom wall above the urinal, someone had scratched I FUCKED YOUR MOTHER. What a barbaric country, no class. He took out a pen from his sports jacket and crossed the vulgarity out, zipped up, washed his hands, and took a look at himself in the mirror.

"Estás listo cabrón?"

Back in the Suburban, Don Luis asked Juanita how much longer to Rancho Maravilloso. He instructed her to wake him in thirty minutes, drifted off, intending to be fresh and alert for his meeting with Jenkins. Polanco wanted a report later tonight, and he would not disappoint.

Arriving at the sales office next to some models, Don Luis put a mint in his mouth and hopped out. The area was beautiful, but remote and far from any amenities one would need for daily living. Maybe that was the point, Don Luis thought, rich gringos pretending they were frontiersmen.

"Are you here for the meeting?"

The question came from a mid-thirties blonde, attractive but with too much make-up. Typical gringa trying too hard. Juanita answered for him.

"Don Luis is a little early, yes. Are the models open? He would like to take a look."

"Of course, let me give you the tour."

Don Luis gave Juanita a look.

"No, that won't be necessary, ma'am."

"Well, okay, I'll be inside if you need me. Have fun, guys!"

This was another thing that bugged Don Luis, unasked for informal manners. *Guys?* He told Juanita to wait outside for Jenkins while he sniffed around. The models were nice in a garish way, expensive finishes the wealthy expected, but all the granite countertops and jacuzzi tubs in the world could not hide the fact that the houses were built out of sticks, chicken wire, and mud. He figured they would last fifty years max, ridiculous for the price.

Out back, beyond the patio, he saw where they'd cleared the desert for a golf course, sodding a few holes with bright, green grass. Was that to impress him, he wondered? Where was the source of water—if not today, then twenty years from now? He walked back inside, and noticed the floor plan had two master suites. Of course, he chuckled, these rich old Anglos can't stand one another. He stopped to stare at the gas fireplace, another fake gimmick in a country full of them.

Pinche gringos!

"Qué opina usted? Es una hermosa vista, no?"

Turning around, there he was. The grand cacique of Southern Arizona.

"Señor Jenkins, a pleasure to meet you, sir."

"Should we go outside? You never know who might be listening."

"Mande?"

"Oh, that's right. Hablamos español, no hay problema."

The meeting went like Don Luis expected. He mostly listened as they walked along the fairway. The old man needed phantom buyers for the sub-division, real estate was down all across the country. These would be retirement homes for wealthy snowbirds, but no one wanted to be first in line. He already had the banks and mortgage companies set up to receive the funds, refinance the loans, then send the money wherever Polanco wanted. For a major commitment, he would not charge any fee for washing the money. It was "win win," as the gringos say. He had refused to do business with the other fellows, and it might have cost him the life of his grandson, who'd brought the Sinaloans to him in a most unfortunate way. He wanted revenge for that, an eye for an eye, whoever was responsible must suffer. Don Luis tried to dissuade him.

"Familia y negocios, no es una buena mezcla."

Jenkins stopped walking and grabbed Don Luis' arm.

"I need this done—*ellos me violaron*—they violated me."

Don Luis didn't bother to argue, he knew it would do little good. Polanco wanted to maintain their relationships in the Southwest, and pleasing the old gringo was *no pasa nada*, no big deal. His boss and Jenkins went way back, both survivors in a business where turnover was high. They probably vacationed together for all he knew.

As Juanita drove him to his hotel, Don Luis had a bad feeling about it all. They were a bunch of cowboys up here, reckless, immature. Polanco's Tucson associate Nestor García was not trustworthy, and probably had set the grandson up. He felt no real need to get to the bottom of it, only to find an amicable solution. He decided he would start with Nestor, then deal with the interlopers from Sinaloa if necessary.

CHAPTER 24

arlowe dreamed of La Española every night, always just out of reach, no way to connect. She would feign interest in whatever he was saying, usually something involving movement: a plane to catch, a rental car to return, a gig to play. In a way he was thankful for finding the corpse; it gave him some relief for his aching heart. He knew in all likelihood the marriage was over—how could it not be? Regardless, he still couldn't shake the idea of winning her back. She hated his addiction to drugs and alcohol, his inability to maintain a balanced lifestyle. He was a drunk and a junkie, a lousy lover, a broke-ass loser. She was a fabulous beauty, smart as hell with a poet's soul.

Who was he kidding?

Continuing to use the den, he couldn't bear sleeping in the master bedroom with its king-sized bed. Retiring at midnight, he would wake at 4 a.m., the drinker's hour, and wonder what she was doing nine hours ahead. Unable to fall back asleep, he took refuge in crime novels: Thompson, Willeford, Cain, MacDonald. He easily inserted himself into the plots—hell, he was living a pretty good one himself. Writing fiction was a deep ambition, but the few times he tried he couldn't even get started. Songs came easy, though. He was cursed—caught in the wrong game, the wrong era, a ham-fisted guitar player getting by on bullshit.

Marlowe woke at dawn and thought about sneaking in nine, but instead took the mountain bike out for a spin before his meeting with Chavez. Taking his usual Indian Ridge route down to the wash, he remembered a way into Tucson Country Club through a mesquite bosque. This is where he got his first stinky finger, making out with cute chicks after smoking loads of buttweed and downing warm quarts of shitty beer. It was all so sweet and innocent back then, before AIDS spread its terror.

The bosque was now built up with houses, but sure enough at the end of Potawatomi there was a gap in the fence to allow walkers and cyclists through, albeit with a sign saying for Tucson Country Club Estates residents only. Marlowe sneered and felt the same old rush sneaking into the forbidden kingdom. Picking up speed, he passed an elderly couple out walking their corgis; he could feel their cold stares.

Go fuck yourselves.

The luscious golf course on his right, he made his way along East Miramar until coming upon Jenkins' house. Out front was an old Corolla and the beat-up white Econoline he'd been snatched in. He felt the still tender lump on his head and kept going, but after a few minutes turned around to get another look. Coming back, he saw another vehicle now parked behind the van: Nestor's pickup with the bright yellow "The Thing" bumper sticker.

No fucking way.

Looking at his watch and feeling anxious, Marlowe nearly crashed into a mailbox. He headed home to shower before his breakfast with Chavez. Pedaling hard uphill, he couldn't wait to spill his guts. He wasn't a tough guy, or a loyal friend—just another slacker in a city full of them. It was time to come clean and face the awful music that was his life. Coming around the last corner into his cul-de-sac, Marlowe slammed on the brakes. Parked right in front of the duplex was Nestor's pickup.

Fuck!

Feigning calm, Marlowe got off the bike and walked it into the carport, where Nestor was sitting on the hood of the Montego, smoking a cigarette.

"Marlowe! There you are! For a second I thought you were hiding inside, avoiding your old pal."

Dizzy with fear, sweating through his shirt, Marlowe put the bike in the storage room, then grabbed a screwdriver from a tool bucket. He came out with it firmly in hand, feeling an electric buzz. Nestor hopped off the hood with a grin.

"Ain't you gonna give me a hug?"

Marlowe plunged the screwdriver into Nestor's gut, up to the hilt. Nestor groaned, looking down at the black and yellow Stanley grip.

"Jesus, Marlowe, that wasn't very nice."

The wound bled down Nestor's shirt, and splattered the concrete. He reached for Marlowe, who stepped back, avoiding his grasp. Nestor lurched toward his truck, whimpering as he opened the door and crawled up into the cab. The starter grinded once before the motor turned over with a shudder.

"Okay, well, I don't know why you did that, but you're gonna pay."

The pickup pulled around and roared off, Nestor slumped behind the wheel. The mocking accordion of a Los Tigres del Norte classic trailed behind . . .

La traición y el contrabando
Son cosas incompartidas

CHAPTER 25

"**Y**ou did what?"

Eating ravenously, Chavez had a piece of egg stuck to his lip Marlowe tried to ignore. The clinically clean and brightly lit Robert's was full of diners chattering like birds, while grimly determined staff conducted traffic. The unlikely twosome occupied the last booth in the rear, eating fried eggs and corned-beef hash liberally dashed with Tabasco.

"Stabbed him in the belly with a screwdriver."

"*Hijole!* Was he threatening you?"

"No . . . yes—well, not exactly. You ever read *The Stranger* by Camus?"

"Huh? I'm a science-fiction nerd, *Strangers in a Strange Land*, yes."

"It felt like I was detached from my body, that I was watching myself do it. He showed up after I saw his truck at Jenkins' house."

"Jenkins? What the hell were you doing there?"

"I was on my bike, just getting some exercise. When I got back to my place Nestor was waiting in the carport. I put the bike away, grabbed a screwdriver, and stabbed him with it."

"What did he do then?"

"Got in his truck and left."

Lost in thought, Chavez went back to his meal. Marlowe tried to eat, but his mouth was too dry. The coffee wasn't helping his anxiety either. Chavez finished up, using one last piece of toast to soak up congealed yolk, then held up his empty cup for the waitress to see.

"You think you killed him—was there a lot of blood?"

"Dunno, it was dripping some but not gushing out."

"Tell me why you're friends with this guy again?"

Marlowe stared out the front window at some passing clouds. The soft morning light a calm ocean blue.

"Look, it's complicated. I was in a band, and we had a party house. He used to come over curious about the scene. We let him sleep on the couch—it was all very innocent."

"You didn't know he's a sociopath?"

"There were signs, but we all had demons—if not, we'd be in college like all the other middle-class kids. We were just into playing music, doing drugs, fucking girls."

Chavez felt himself getting angry—must be nice to be so spoiled. He'd been busting his ass in the Air Force at that age.

"All right, I'll have someone call around to the emergency rooms, see if he shows. In the meantime, you're gonna tell me everything you know about George, his grandfather, Nestor, all of it. If I think you're holding anything back, I'm gonna take you in as a suspect, understand?"

Marlowe suddenly felt hungry and piled some cold eggs and hash onto a piece of rye and took a large bite. Washing it down with lukewarm coffee, he looked Chavez in the eye and nodded.

"The whole thing started when I clubbed down to an 8 but caught it pure and flew the green, right into that fucking trap."

CHAPTER 26

D
on Luis woke up early and took a walk around the hotel. He liked this
Arizona Inn, graceful grounds with little adobe bungalows spaced here
and there. It reminded him of home, Cuernavaca, a city of gardens.
Growing up, he was on the other side of the high walls the wealthy topped
with broken glass, but now he was inside their world and would never be
denied again. He lingered to admire the pool area and resisted picking up
a skimmer to remove a few leaves floating around. Making his way back to
his bungalow, he nodded at a young Mexican kid delivering room service,
and noticed two tennis courts set back behind some hedges—just what he
needed.

He called the desk, delighted to be greeted in Spanish. He asked if they
had a pro available for a tennis lesson. Absolutely, how about in thirty minutes? He put on a pair of shorts, Adidas shoes, and a white collared cotton
shirt from a suitcase Juanita had brought, then made his way to the courts.
Waiting at the gate with two rackets was the pro, a young tanned kid with
an awkward smile. He explained in halting Spanish that he was a student at
the university, played on the team, and did this for beer money. Don Luis
smiled, patted him on the back, and with a sweeping gesture indicated they
should move to the court.

Like all good players, they started at half court, hitting little half volleys
back and forth. Slowly they inched back until they were behind the baselines,
smacking full ground strokes. Don Luis' timing was off from all the travel,
but he felt wonderful out practicing with a player much better than himself.
He always sought out his superiors, be it in business or pleasure. There was
no other way to live—either you kept learning or you died.

After forty minutes, a court phone rang shrilly, interrupting their practice.
The kid looked at Don Luis, who shrugged and nodded for him to answer.
Drinking water from a fountain, Don Luis watched as the kid motioned him

over and handed him the receiver, before walking away to allow for some privacy.

"Dígame?"

Don Luis listened attentively for a few minutes. It was Juanita. There was a problem with the associate Nestor the halcón—he needed medical attention. Don Luis swore, barked a few instructions, then hung up.

Pinche cowboys!

Peeling a hundred bucks off his roll, Don Luis handed it to the kid for a tip, who explained the court fee and lesson would be added to his bill at checkout.

"Gracias, mister, sorry we got cut short. You have very good footwork, *un buen juego de pies.* Keep working on getting into the right position to hit those winners."

Don Luis grinned and handed back the racket.

"*Si, el tenis y la vida,* how you say? One and the same."

Don Luis walked back to his bungalow and watched a roadrunner dart across a croquet lawn set up for the guests. He reminded himself he was here on a mission, to mend fences, to avoid a costly turf war. There were only so many plazas available, and Nogales was a prize. He could not afford to chunk this particular ball into the net.

CHAPTER 27

J enkins, George, Nestor, Paco, Marlowe, Roy—what a shit show, a *desmadre* of epic proportions. Chavez didn't like where the case was heading, in particular Nestor's involvement with Jenkins. Sitting at his desk downtown, he drew a flow chart just out of habit. The squad's secretary, Joyce, had called all the emergency rooms within a hundred miles, but no incidents with screwdrivers, no stabbings, nada. Looking down at the circled names and arrows pointing to and fro, Chavez tried to grasp what it all meant.

The old man was not just a beloved upstanding Tucsonan, he *was* Tucson. A founder of "The Sunshine Club," he'd been instrumental in turning this sleepy desert town into a major tourist destination. He was also largely responsible for ripping the heart out of the Mexican community, after murdering one of their own. *La Calle* was where on Saturdays Chavez's *abuela* took him to shop for clothes, then off to see a Mexican movie at La Placita Theater. Slurping raspados and playing with friends and neighbors, Chavez had some of his fondest memories there as a child. Until one day it all disappeared, replaced by the cold concrete and glass of a convention center. The civic boosters told all sorts of lies to themselves and the public to claim this was progress, but really what they did was unforgivable, creating a divide between Anglo and Mexican that could never be fully bridged. Now here was Jenkins, knee-deep in what exactly? Drug dealing? Nah. Money laundering? Possibly. How the hell did he know Nestor?

Remembering Marta, Chavez got out the phone book and looked her up. She wasn't listed, but her nephew Chuy was. Chavez had played Little League with him when they were kids. Chuy answered on the third ring, and after catching up with the latest gossip, gave Chavez Marta's number. It was her day off, fortunately, and she agreed to meet him at her home in an hour.

Heading downstairs, Chavez decided to walk the few blocks to where Marta lived in El Hoyo. This was all that was left of the old neighborhood, now overrun with self-satisfied gringos renovating 19th-century adobe homes and rowhouses. Passing El Minuto Cafe then El Tiradito shrine, Chavez crossed himself out of habit and wiped his brow in the heat. He had mixed emotions about the gentrification—it wasn't all bad; still the Anglos were doing something that had been denied to his community: preserving history. He was as tired of the do-gooders as he was of the abject racists—both were full of shit.

He found Marta's casa behind Carrillo Elementary's playground, where he played kickball as a kid. He knocked on the door, anxious to get out of the sun. She answered with a smile, then poured him a cool glass of *limonada* and gestured for him to sit in an old pigskin Equipale chair. On the walls were photos of family and friends, as well as a striking mosaic of Guadalupe framed in mesquite. Marta was one of the few El Hoyo holdouts, her widow's exemption kept the rising property taxes at bay that forced so many of her old neighbors to move. After a few pleasantries, Chavez got down to business.

"Now Marta, anything you say I will keep confidential. I'm interested in a guy that drives an old pickup—Nestor is his name. I have information that he visits your employer Jenkins. What can you tell me about him?"

Marta fingered her rosary and thought for a moment. Deciding something, her words rushed out.

"He is a bad man. He comes over once a month, acts like he owns the place. Señor Jenkins always sees him in the den, with the door locked."

"What do they talk about?"

"I have no idea, but after he leaves Señor Jenkins becomes extra quiet, sad. It's hard to explain. I asked Roy about him once, and he made the sign of a gun with his hand, pointed it at my head and pulled the trigger. Told me to mind my own business."

"What do you think of Roy?"

"He's also a bad man, an ex-con, but he's loyal to Señor Jenkins, works hard."

"You ever hear stories about Jenkins having another family?"

Marta stared at Guadalupe, mulling it over again.

"Yes, there have always been rumors, *chismes en el barrio*. If you look closely at Nestor, he has the same green eyes as Señor Jenkins, like *tapatíos*, and they're both tall and—what's the word? Lanky. I always wondered if they were related. I know it sounds crazy, but that's *mi intuición*, a mother's intuition."

Chavez stayed quiet and chewed on an ice cube. It made total sense, and that worried him. He thanked her for her time, gave her a hug and a peck on each cheek, and walked back to his office. Stopping at El Tiradito shrine, he prayed for strength and wisdom, lighting a candle with a wooden match he found in the dirt. *Abuela's* voice found him again.

De tal palo tal astilla, from the log comes the splinter, like father like son.

CHAPTER 28

After a quick shower, Don Luis changed clothes and met Juanita in the lobby. Asking for two coffees to go, they soon were on I-19 heading south to Tubac, the highway strangely marked in metric as if they were already back in Mexico.

Passing the brilliant lime-washed white of San Xavier Mission, Don Luis made a note to see it up close. He was a student of the different Catholic orders and their influence in Mexico. He thought about the long, perilous journey from here to San Francisco, Juan Bautista de Anza establishing the route in only five months. Don Luis admired *and* hated the Spanish, their legal institutions and vestigial oligarchy cursed Mexico to this day. The Puritans were no better, but at least the Spanish didn't try to exterminate the natives, enslaving them instead. The Aztecs themselves came to the Valley of Mexico from somewhere in the north, arriving just a few centuries before the Spanish. Soon, the newcomers took it over, crazed priests sacrificing children to make it rain. At the same time in England, street urchins were hanged for stealing a loaf of bread, displaying the power of the Crown. What was the difference?

Turning east into Tubac, they arrived at a rambling adobe ranch house, set well back back from the golf course. Don Luis hopped out and signaled for Juanita to follow. In the driveway sat an old classic Ford 150, with a garish yellow bumper sticker advertising "The Thing." Nearby was a late-model Chevy Silverado with a factory-installed tow package, typical rancher vehicle. The doorbell was answered by a gruff, chiseled-faced Anglo, wearing a snap-button western shirt, jeans, cowboy hat, and roper boots.

"Don Luis, I presume. My name is Carl. Your boy is in the back, just getting ready to work on him."

Juanita began to translate, but Don Luis waved her off, having understood most of it.

The house was decorated in classic Southwestern style, rough-cut beams and smooth plaster walls, sunken living room with an old leather couch, and two club chairs facing a stone fireplace. No different from that of a wealthy rancher from El Bajío, Don Luis thought. Almost all cattle ranching techniques and culture came from Mexico, but few gringos knew that. Passing the Saltillo-tiled kitchen, with its own raised fireplace to grill meat, they headed out the rear door to a detached prefab metal building next to a few cattle-holding pens.

"Don't know if they told ya, but I ain't no MD—I'm a vet. But people are animals, too, I reckon. I've seen pretty much everything, here and back in 'Nam, where I was a medic."

Don Luis smiled as Juanita translated.

"You'd be surprised the trouble a range steer can get into, and what can happen to a fuckin' new guy walking point. Your boy's injury reminds me of a punji stick wound."

Opening the door to the clinic, they entered to find a groaning Nestor lying on a metal examination table, scrunched up in the fetal position.

"Glad you showed up when you did—he ain't gonna like it when I pull that out. Why don't you each take one of his arms and hold him down on his back. Hopefully he won't jerk too much or kick me in the nuts like that goddamn horse did last week."

Don Luis nodded grimly. Inside he was amused, but polite enough not to show it. He asked for two lab coats to protect their clothes from the blood that was already smeared on the cold table.

"Good idea. It didn't hit an artery or anything vital or he'd be dead, but could get messy all the same. I haven't given him anything for the pain because he showed up with constricted pupils—don't want him to overdose. Okay, hold him tight."

Nestor's eyes got wide as they pinned him on his back. Don Luis noticed their green hue and thought of Jenkins—were they related somehow?

"Alright, uno, dos, tres . . ."

Screwdriver yanked out, Nestor screamed a high-pitched wail that got all the neighborhood dogs barking. The vet quickly gave him a rubber chew toy to bite down on.

"Jesus, that'll raise the dead. Alright, let me clean that wound out."

Using a turkey-baster–sized syringe, Carl squirted saline in the wound while mopping up blood. Nestor wriggled and squirmed, tears running down his cheeks. He finally spat the rubber bone out, and hissed like a snake.

"*Chinga tu madre cabrón!* Give me something or I'll rip your head off!"

Don Luis nodded okay. The vet went to a steel cabinet, got out a vial and syringe, and hit Nestor in a vein, making him slump in relief.

"Oh, that's good, feels like a cold spoon in the back of my throat."

"You're lucky to feel anything at all with your habit."

Nestor flashed a sick grin . . .

"What habit, doc? And who the fuck is this guy?"

Don Luis slapped him hard across the face, then gave him a backhand as well.

"*Soy Don Luis, tu jefe pendejo*, understand?"

Nestor laid back, defeated, as the vet finished up, putting a clean dressing on his wound.

"Looks like y'all could use some privacy. He'll want to clean it out twice a day—gonna hurt like hell, but he seems to do his own pain management. I'll give him some antibiotics, as well—hog dosage should work. I'll be in the house if you need me."

Nestor spat blood on the floor from biting his tongue, then sighed as the old cowboy took his leave.

"*Lo siento*, boss, I hurt so bad."

"Okay, listen to me, you tell me everything. How *el nieto de Jenkins* died, todo. *Si creo que estás mintiendo, te mataré.*"

Don Luis picked up the screwdriver, glancing at Juanita.

"If he thinks you're lying, he's gonna shove it back in."

Nestor's jaw clenched, but sister morphine was still embracing him like a warm blanket.

"*Fue un accidente. Tengo que hablar* in English—my Spanish sucks."

Of course it does, thought Don Luis, you *pinche pocho*. But after listening to his long twisted tale, he couldn't judge him too harshly. The story was so stupid it had to be true—only a fool would make up something so banal. He told Nestor to get straight and rest for a few days, then be ready to help clean this mess up. On the way out, they found Carl drinking coffee in the kitchen. Don Luis tried to pay him from his wad, but Carl waved him off.

"Much obliged to your outfit, keeping my boy safe up in Florence. I told him he'd get nabbed one day, running those loads, but he just wouldn't listen. He gave up on the cattle business—hell, can't blame him for that; it's never been easy. Proud he held his mud, though. He's doing his time like a man. Thank god my Sara didn't live to see her son in prison."

Listening to the translation, Don Luis stuck out his hand and they shook.

"Gracias, Carl. La organización no forget."

Some gringos were okay, Don Luis thought. This man would make a good neighbor. On the ride back, deep purple cumulus clouds rolled in for a late-season monsoon. The first drops hit the windshield as Juanita pulled up to the hotel, and by the time Don Luis made it to his bungalow, he was drenched head to toe.

CHAPTER 29

Still squirrelly after breakfast with Chavez, anxious about Nestor, Marlowe hit a noon meeting at a new-age bookstore in Monterey Village. One of the first eastside shopping centers, this was where civilization began when he was a kid. Now Speedway and Wilmot was the center of town, with endless sprawl right up to the base of the Rincon Mountains.

After the obligatory readings from the literature, Marlowe listened to addicts talk about whatever was giving them trouble, or helping them stay clean. Marlowe rarely shared—hell, he didn't know these people and wouldn't get high with them if he did. Still, there was something to this "one addict helping another" business; he always felt calmer and less dope-obsessed after a meeting. As one old-timer put it, if you don't pick up, the rest was just conversation. That was good to know because Marlowe had no *higher power* to call upon, just a lower one he wanted to keep far, far away.

The main problem was Marlowe wasn't looking for a brand-new life, just a canoe to cross the river. The way the program used fear to keep people sober was wrong in his view, and the warmed-over Oxford Group spiritualism corny as fuck. Marlowe also didn't believe in the disease model—to him it was a cop-out. Sure, you could get tissue-dependent, and withdrawal *was* hellish and often required medical supervision, but kicking was therapeutic, and once detoxed an addict could reasonably make some life choices, good or bad. Marlowe was just trying to do the next right move, like another old-timer had suggested. The whole "jails, institutions, and death" spiel he could do without. Most people got themselves out of addictive behaviors on their own—they didn't need 12 steps to guide them to a saner life.

Feeling better after a reluctant hug or two, Marlowe drove to Randolph to knock it around. He was nearly out of money, the last publishing advance dwindling away on green fees, gasoline, and burritos. Strangely, he didn't care; he was tired of the music jizz after a decade of wagging his weenie.

Recently he'd heard a new term for folk, blues, and country: *Americana*. Something about it smelled wrong, like the staged Civil War photos of Mathew Brady. Lacing up his golf shoes, Marlowe mused there was a time and place for everything, and rock 'n' roll was—if not dead—firmly in its tertiary stage.

He remembered a slick Texas producer showing up at the offices of Trash Records. Wearing a sharkskin suit and bullshitting with the label president, the tall, skinny prick pontificated about who was worthy of his time. It was just one stop that day among A&R departments all over town. The dude let it be known he'd be working for the labels, not the bands. Marlowe knew then that punk rock was over—the vultures had arrived.

A few months later, he ran into that same used-car salesman on the roof-top of a music publisher, a party celebrating the genius of Willie Dixon. Fucker had an English rock star in tow, showing him off like a pedigreed dog. Why tea-bags fell so hard for the L.A. myth Marlowe could never under-stand, maybe because they never ventured east of Western Avenue. If they had, they'd realize L.A. wasn't at all what they imagined, neither dream nor fantasy, but a real place where most barely scraped by working in sweatshops, construction, light manufacturing, service industry, and restaurants.

Regardless, Marlowe missed L.A. and his first love, Robin, almost as much as La Española. Why did he shit on all he held dear? It had to be more than drugs, some sort of curse like Robert Johnson and his hellhounds. Shutting the Montego's trunk, Marlowe grabbed his sticks and walked to the course like a pilgrim on his way to Jericho. If salvation was impossible, then he'd settle for a round of par.

The Randolph starter recognized Marlowe and put him out with a scratch golfer. It was one of those links afternoons where the world stopped; all that mattered was the journey lying right before them. The noise of nearby cars and trucks disappeared, replaced by birds and cicadas, along with the occa-sional sprinkler head watering a brown spot.

Paradise.

There's a difference between a golfer and someone who merely plays golf. This guy said little, even his age was difficult to tell—fifty? Face deeply tanned, when he took his glove off to putt, his left hand was so pale it nearly blinded Marlowe. His short game was impeccable and how he scored as low as he did. Knowing he could get up and down from almost anywhere, it took pressure off his mid-game, and he went after all the pins except when it was just ridiculous to try. He also hit fairways religiously, rarely getting into trouble off the tee. Marlowe played his normal better-than-a-hacker, but-not-quite-yet-a-player game, and tried to absorb the magic he was witnessing. He had no idea what his own score was, and when he managed to save par after a bad drive on 18, the golfer commented with a Scottish brogue.

"Well done, laddie, you broke 80."

Driving home, Marlowe felt a deep calm he'd only known before on drugs. He realized he didn't even know what *normal* was, since he started getting wasted on a daily basis back in junior high. He thought of La Española—why did she marry someone so obviously fucked up? What right did he have to want her back, since he didn't even know who the fuck he was? Regardless, he felt a deep longing, a string-theory connection of their life together, as if the future had already happened and was now folded back on itself.

Crazy.

After scoring an Eegee's sub and wolfing it down for dinner, Marlowe took refuge in Ben Hogan's *Five Lessons*. The Hawk's description of pronation and supination mystified him—what the fuck was this man talking about? Marlowe started to nod off in a big leather chair, watching the Wildcats play basketball against UCLA. Taking the book to bed, he tried to figure where he stood. Nestor would be back for revenge, no doubt about it. Jenkins probably wanted his ass, too—and did Chavez really believe him? He laid down and opened *Five Lessons* to a random page, his eyes immediately drawn to a bit of sage advice:

The most important shot in golf is the next one.

If he could break 80, he could get himself through this absurdity. All he needed was a bit of luck, and to not make things worse.

One shot at a time.

CHAPTER 30

C havez went back to surveilling the Goat Lady, figuring Nestor would eventually show to keep the pain in check. He still didn't understand why Marlowe had stabbed him—funny way to treat your friend. Paco should have known where to find Nestor, but insisted that he came and went like the wind. Nothing in this fucking case made sense, Chavez thought; it was worse than a bullshit TV police procedural. Too many coincidences and irrational explanations.

Drinking tepid coffee a block from the Goat Lady's house, Chavez kept the windows down so he wouldn't bake. A few neighbors gave him the eye, but they were used to cops watching the dope house. Feeling sleepy, he riffed on Jenkins and his relationship with Nestor. His bastard grandson? Did George know? Probably. What about Roy? Jenkins was scared of something—blackmail? And what the fuck was a washed-up musician doing in all this? Just bad luck? Chavez believed Marlowe and Paco up to a point, but would need more proof. Why didn't Marlowe just report the body when he found it? He'd be free and clear by now.

Chavez drifted off, and dreamed of Carmen in a slinky negligee. They were drinking champagne after coitus bliss, madly in love and newly married. The honeymoon suite looked upon a beach, the sound of crashing surf lulling them to sleep. Sighing, he was rudely awakened by someone rapping on his windshield.

"Hey, Mr. Officer, you gonna park here all day?"

Chavez opened an eye, a tweaker skater stared at him, wearing a Flipside T-shirt and holding his board.

"Why are you harassing us, *ese*? Why don't you find some real criminals up in the Foothills?"

Chavez was just gonna laugh when he saw Nestor's truck pull up to the Goat Lady's house.

"Scram, punk, before I get out and beat your ass."

Flipping Chavez off, the budding anarchist dropped his deck to the sidewalk and skedaddled. Chavez watched Nestor hobble down out of his truck, shuffling around to the back of the house while holding his side.

Hijole! Marlowe really did stick him good!

Chavez squirmed with impatience. He watched Nestor reappear a half-hour later, still moving slow but no longer clutching his side, probably fixed inside after buying some dope. Not wanting to alert the Goat Lady, he followed Nestor's truck a few blocks before lighting him up. He should have called for backup, but still wanted the freedom to run the case as he saw fit—fuck the Lieutenant.

Getting out with his gun drawn, Chavez approached the cab like a coyote sniffing a rattlesnake. Nestor stared straight ahead, hands at 10 and 2 on the wheel.

"That's good, *cabrón*, keep 'em right there."

Chavez put his left elbow on top of the door like he was at a bar, his weapon in his right hand.

"Nestor, Nestor García."

"No, I'm Guillermo, his brother—you want to see my ID?"

"That won't be necessary, Nestor. Do you know who I am?"

"No idea, some narc I imagine."

"Homicide."

"Homicide? Who died?"

"George Jenkins."

"Yeah, I read about that."

"You must feel bad."

"Bad? About some rich white boy?"

Nestor's breathing got a little more rapid, eyes pinned like lasers, breath fetid like a dog's.

"Didn't you know him?"

"How would I know that *pinche gabacho*?"

"What about the old man, his grandfather?"

"What, you think I'm his pool guy or something? How would I know any of those people?"

"What about Marlowe, Marlowe Billings?"

"The musician? Sure, I know him—we used to hang out a little. He's not mixed up in this, is he?"

"You tell me."

"Last I heard he was living in Spain with some chica."

"When was the last time you saw him?"

"I don't know—a few years back in L.A., I guess. Hey, am I under arrest 'cause if I ain't I'd really like to be on my way."

"If you're thinking about *venganza*, best put it out of your mind."

"Revenge? Against who? For what?"

"For that hole in your belly, looks like it's leaking a little."

Nestor glanced down at the spreading red flower and smiled.

"Oh, *no pasa nada*, just a scratch."

"Must have hurt like hell—now why would an old friend do something like that?"

"Look, I'm gonna take my right hand off this wheel and turn on the ignition. I suggest you back up so I don't run over your foot. If you're gonna shoot me, make it count—I've had enough bullshit for one week."

"Sure, sure, have a nice day and all that. Surprised you don't remember me—the cop that arrested you for shooting that poor dude in the face? He lost his vision and killed himself a few years later."

Nestor grinned.

"Well, shit happens, as they say. I thought I recognized you. I knew your cousin Johnny—too bad he was such a lightweight and OD'd."

Chavez brought his weapon up and held it to Nestor's temple.

"Remember what I said—leave Marlowe alone."

Chavez backed away and gestured with his left hand, a torero waving a bull through to perdition. Nestor cranked the starter and rumbled off, flipping a bird out the window as a final adiós. Chavez stared at the bright yellow "The Thing" bumper sticker and smirked.

Did they really have Pancho Villa's car there? One day he just had to find out.

CHAPTER 31

Don Luis lounged by Arizona Inn's understated black-bottom pool and watched an old wrinkled prune swim laps. She hadn't even said good morning to him, rude bitch. The resident roadrunner was more polite and gave him a cackle before snagging a lizard. Don Luis was enjoying this place, restrained elegance in the middle of the city. He looked forward to getting another tennis lesson, but business before pleasure, as the gringos say.

He tried to put himself in Jenkins' shoes—what motivated him? A city father, upstanding citizen, but with secrets that would soil his legacy. Nestor's claim of being the bastard great-grandchild of Jenkins' father rang true—how else would he know the man? Spoiled *nieto* George, using his *abuelo's* name to lure in a rival cartel—yeah, that made sense. Jenkins' godson Roy, promising distribution through his prison biker connections, okay. But meth, really? Wasn't coke lucrative enough? He'd heard rumors of shipments of precursor chemicals shipped into Lázaro Cárdenas from China—was Sinaloa moving away from the Colombians? Meth made sense in countries where people were working 16-hour days, but the United States? And this *pinche* musician, Marlowe Billings, innocent but up to his neck in shit—how could that be?

Sipping an iced tea, Don Luis remembered a lesson learned from a wealthy *Porteño* long ago: The simplest, least-complicated solution was usually the correct one. The answer to any puzzle was most likely right under your nose. He thought of the first Catholic president, Kennedy, shot down like a dog in Texas. The Mafia? The CIA? The Cubans? Or just that loser Oswald, wanting fame and glory. It was so easy to get off track, to believe in fantasy to make sense of a chaotic world. Stick with the facts, reality is what's observable. Everything else is just conjecture.

He would have to handle Jenkins without humiliating him—that was clear. Had the old man gone to the Sinaloans to invest in Rancho Maravilloso? Did they turn him down and set George up? What about Nestor, playing both sides of the street? Was he working for Sinaloa, too? This homicide cop, some *cabrón* named Chavez—could he be bought off? And Paco the greenskeeper, just a reluctant mule as Nestor claimed? Maybe he'd gotten ambitious, saw the stash of money his aunt kept in her closet and wanted some for himself? Start moving a little weight for Sinaloa, get Nestor off his back? Paco was a good place to start, validate Nestor's story, figure shit out before any killing starts. The one thing he *did* believe was how George died, a fitting end for such an asshole. Whatever the case, the Nogales plaza had to stay in Polanco's control—by any means necessary, as some bad-ass *cabrón* once put it.

Chewing on a piece of ice, Don Luis turned his head to avoid staring at the *vieja* exiting the pool. She gave him a withering look before wrapping herself in a towel and shuffling off to her bungalow. Sometimes he felt like a priest, but instead of prescribing devotions for unfortunate behaviors, he decided who lived and died. His own continued existence was predicated on the decisions he made. At some point, a fatal mistake would be made—of that he was certain. Until then, he was going to enjoy life as best he could, he was a hundred percent Mexican after all. Why fret about the inevitable? Maybe they weren't *la raza cósmica* as Fuentes proclaimed, but at least they weren't gringos full of neurosis and fear.

CHAPTER 32

arlowe didn't know Nestor would be at Grum's, but he *knew*. He knocked, heard murmurs inside, then saw a curtain crack giving him the once over. The door finally opened and Grum waved him in. Nestor was slumped in a chair watching *Oprah*, didn't even turn his head. Marlowe sat on the couch next to Grum, who started rolling a joint. The show's theme was taking better care of oneself, giving yourself permission to be happy. The audience laughed as Oprah put herself through some yoga moves with one of the expert guests, the camera zooming in to capture her discomfort. Nestor broke the silence.

"I could do that, if I didn't have a hole in my belly."

The joint went around with Marlowe declining. Everyone chuckled at a Mr. Clean commercial, the bald-headed freak with a hot housewife. Grum piped up.

"You just know he's hitting that."

The show went back to the health benefits of neti pots and coffee enemas. Nestor groaned a couple of times, adjusting his position. Marlowe figured it was time.

"Where's Nestor's pickup?"

"Over at the Boondocks, I won't let him park in front."

Nestor snickered.

"Dude, I'm breakin' parole just having you here."

Nestor hissed.

"Go ahead and ask him."

"Marlowe, Nestor wants to know why you stabbed him."

Marlowe waved the joint off a second time.

"He knows why I stabbed him."

"Nestor, Marlowe says you know why he stabbed you."

"Because he was scared I'd hurt him?"

"Marlowe, were you scared?"

"I guess, the threat is always there because he's a psychotic son of a bitch. My brain broke, I couldn't deal with the stress."

Nestor took a big toke.

"Tell Marlowe I can understand that. Sometimes you just have to lash out at whoever's nearest, but stabbing me in the gut with a screwdriver seems a little extreme, no?"

"You gonna kill me?"

Nestor turned and looked directly at Marlowe.

"No, I promised Grum I wouldn't. Your cop buddy Chavez is worried about that, too, hassling me. We're gonna stick together until I figure out what to do. I shouldn't have got you into this, but after you found George your fate was sealed. I couldn't just ignore the pure chance of that—that would be denying that God exists, that life has no meaning."

"Never took you for a religious sort."

Grum snorted.

"I was an altar boy until they caught me stealing from the alms. The padre demanded a blow job and I spat in his face."

They all chuckled while Oprah got emotional discussing her reluctance to masturbate, raised Southern Baptist and all. The audience giggled nervously when she pulled out a Hitachi Magic Wand.

"Hey, I got one of those for my wife, but she never used it."

Nestor and Grum looked mockingly at Marlowe.

"I thought it was a nice Valentine's gift."

As the credits rolled, Nestor dragged himself up and went into the bathroom to fix.

"You think he's gonna kill me?"

"Nah, he loves you, but I wouldn't stab him again."

In the distance they heard a siren, followed by a neighbor's dog howling. Nestor finally came out, moving slow.

"Okay, Marlowe, we're gonna take a ride in that Mercury of yours. Grum, make sure the Boondocks doesn't tow my truck—here's my keys."

"Will do. You boys have a nice time now, you hear? No more of this bickering."

Nestor raised his shirt to look at the dressing on his wound, flashing the grip of a pistol tucked into his pants.

"Oh, I don't think Marlowe's gonna give me any more trouble. He only lost his cool there for a spell, right, *ese*?"

"It was a preternatural event."

"If you say so, well, but I think you just don't want to face your destiny."

"Who does?"

"Jesus showed the way, took it like a man."

Grum opened the front door and let his friends pass. Momentarily blind, Nestor put his hand on Marlowe's shoulder to lead him forward and into the light.

CHAPTER 33

Back at his desk, Chavez called the old gringo and requested a meeting. Jenkins said he'd be downtown later for a bank conference, and they could meet at El Charro at five. Oddly, he didn't ask if Chavez had any new information or why he wanted to talk in person. Chavez hung up and flashed back on one of his favorite shows as a kid: *Columbo*. This was a lost episode, with some old great like Melvyn Douglas playing Jenkins. He remembered Carmen loved the show, and his heart grew heavy. Was it really over between them? He picked up the phone to talk, but got her voicemail instead.

"Hola, guapa, it's me, the stupid cop. Was just thinking about your favorite TV show. If I get a frumpy raincoat, can I come visit? Let me know."

Having made the first move, he felt immediately better. Why do we torture ourselves? Stupid pride is all, machismo. Chavez wanted a family, and Carmen would be a wonderful person to start one with. He decided that after he wrapped up this case, he would put the required time and effort in to pursue her. If she turned him down, then at least he wouldn't kick himself later for not trying. It wasn't like he was young anymore; the job had aged him more than he wanted to admit.

Chavez tried to sneak out of the office before the Jenkins meeting, but the Lieutenant waved at him wanting an update. Chavez shrugged, pointing to his watch. The Lieutenant held up an index finger and mouthed *one week, you got one week.*

Chavez hit wedges at El Rio for an hour, then got to El Charro a few minutes before five. He found Jenkins in the bar drinking a Paloma and snacking on *cacahuates japoneses*. Chavez ordered the same and they retired to a private room, away from prying ears. The old man moved slow, but still had good posture, as if a steel rod went down his spine.

"So, Detective, what do you have for me?"

Chavez stared at his drink and thought of the show again—how would Columbo play it?

"*Señor Jenkins, cómo conoce a Nestor García?*"

The old man's face hardened, then sagged. He took a gulp and sighed.

"*Él es el bisnieto de mi padre*, his great-grandson—you must know that by now."

"Was he friends with George?"

"*Friends* is the wrong word—they were *medio primos*, half-cousins I guess. Hell, I don't know what you would call it. George figured it out in high school, going through my desk looking for money. He came across some photos and recognized Nestor. They went to different high schools, but George was already selling drugs and had connections in the barrio—that's how they met. Nestor told me all this later, when he started . . ."

"Extorting you?"

"Wrong word again. Nestor's mother died of cancer when he was a toddler—I doubt he remembers her. His *abuela*, my father's daughter and my half sister, passed soon thereafter. She and I were close. She never threatened to reveal our relationship, although there were always rumors. She had another daughter, who moved to San Antonio decades ago, and a son who died in Vietnam. Nestor is all who's left in Tucson from the Mexican side of the family."

"Family? Is that what they are to you?"

Jenkins stared hard at Chavez.

"What has this got to do with George's murder?"

"You tell me."

"Nestor didn't kill George."

"How do you know that?"

Jenkins grew silent and gazed at a photo of Zapata and Pancho Villa on the wall, sitting together in the National Palace in Mexico City. A waiter poked his head into the room, and Chavez waved him off. The old man finally looked back at Chavez with new resolve.

"Why aren't you looking at that punk who found George, this Marlowe Billings character?"

"I've spoken to him—it was just a coincidence he found George."

Jenkins lowered the hammer.

"Does your lieutenant think so too? A coincidence? I must have a word with him."

Face turning red, Chavez downed the rest of his drink—fuck Columbo.

"Don't try to squeeze me, Señor Jenkins. I haven't leaked anything to the press so far, but I'm not above it. I doubt you're telling me half of what you know about your grandson's death. He was a nasty piece of work—maybe you are, too. I know you killed Eusebio Pérez, and there's no statute of limitations for that. Were you there the day they bulldozed his building? That must have felt good."

"That's not why . . ."

"Sure it is. You grew up downtown, most of your friends were Mexican. You had family there, but you couldn't talk about it. Hell, this restaurant used to be on West Broadway, before it all got leveled so you and your friends could whitewash history and pretend Tucson wasn't Mexican. Look at me, you son-of-a-bitch."

Jenkins kept staring at his drink.

"That will do, Detective. You've now crossed a line I won't forget. I've been straight with you and gave you more respect than you deserve. But now you are acting . . ."

Chavez stood up and sneered down at Jenkins.

"Above my station? Like a white man? I'm not your priest, and I'm sure as hell not your vigilante. I had generals like you in the Air Force, always taking credit, never responsible for anything. They kept bootlickers around, like Roy—yeah, I know about him and his criminal record, too. Maybe this case isn't about poor George at all—it's about you and the deals you've made over the years to keep Tucson growing, feeding the cancer. I wonder what I'll find if I keep digging—more than just Eusebio Pérez's bones I bet."

Jenkins looked up stone cold.

"You have no idea who you're talking to and the forces I can unleash. You had a very simple job, and you failed. Good afternoon, Detective. Any further communication will be through my attorneys."

Chavez walked out of El Charro and shook his head at the line. These people were searching for the soul of a city that didn't exist anymore. He was tired of pretending that a grave injustice hadn't happened, that part of him hadn't been murdered just like Eusebio Pérez.

When he got home he listened to his messages, but Carmen's voice was not to be found. He poured himself a mescal and hit some putts on the carpet to calm down. He thought of Jenkins and stroked one much too firm, shattering the glass tumbler he used as a hole.

Fucking gringos!

CHAPTER 34

They drove west into the sun, the old Ajo highway, listening to the Beach Boys on an oldies station. Brian happy to be in his room, away from the world. Riding shotgun, Nestor didn't say much, nodding in and out. They stopped at a Circle K and bought bread and crackers, canned soup and chili, ibuprofen, bandages, isopropyl alcohol, ten gallons of water, and a case of Gatorade.

"We going camping?"

Nestor stayed quiet and directed Marlowe to hang a left at an unmarked dirt road a few miles from the Kitt Peak exit. Soon they came to a cattle guard and gate. Nestor groaned as he got out to let them through. Marlowe felt oddly calm, didn't know where they were going, but no longer cared what happened to him. Finding George Jenkins wasn't bad luck—it was fate, just like Nestor said. Consequently, it meant everything had already happened— they were only actors in a cosmic play, puppets on a string.

After five more desolate miles, with only a few steers here and there, Nestor told Marlowe to turn right at another dirt road, barely noticeable beyond a majestic crested saguaro. Marlowe took it slow, the path just two ruts in the hard caliche dirt. Soon they came to a small hill, with an abandoned-looking stone cabin at its base. Flushing quail as they got out, Nestor grimaced and told Marlowe to bring the supplies inside. It took a couple trips from the car to the rickety porch, where they stacked it all before Nestor worked the rusty latch and slipped inside.

Despite its outer appearance, the interior was fairly clean and well organized. There was a small metal table with two chairs, a dry sink, some shelves with a Coleman lantern, candles, cans of Sterno, a portable stove, and an old battery-powered radio. In the corner was a small cot, with a rolled-up sleeping bag on top. Nestor immediately went about cooking up a dose, tying off with his belt before hitting a vein on his third try. He slumped in the chair and Marlowe thought maybe he OD'd, but eventually Nestor lifted his head and rasped instructions.

"Okay, that's my last shot. Get the hell out of here before I change my mind. Come back in a week or so. You don't got anything to read, do you?"

Marlowe almost said no, then remembered there was some NA literature he'd thrown in the glove box. He went out to get it, returning to find Nestor laying on the cot, his pistol next to the works on the table.

"Take that shit away, don't want to see it."

"Everything?"

"Leave my piece, don't know if I can kick again."

Marlowe used the NA basic text to sweep the bent spoon, hypodermic, and cotton into a plastic bag, then placed the book next to the gun.

"Make sure you close that gate on the way out," Nestor said. "We have a deal with the rancher who leases this land—if it's open he'll call *la migra*."

"Border Patrol? What for?"

"Don't worry 'bout that, just close the goddamn gate. If anyone tries to fuck with you, don't cooperate. Don't get into a car with anybody, even if they got a gun on ya, or a badge. If something is going down, make sure it happens right there, not someplace else. Don't go back to your place, and don't stay with Grum."

"What the fuck, dude?"

Nestor moaned again.

"Get out of here—they'll be looking for me, not you."

"The cops? Chavez?"

"He's the least of my problems."

"Did you kill George? I need to know."

"Fuck no, he was my milk cow, and my . . . you don't wanna know, Marlowe—it doesn't matter anyway. We're all fucked unless I can get it together. Now get out of here before I shoot your white ass."

Marlowe shut the door softly behind him and wondered whether he'd ever see Nestor again. A week was a long time—a lifetime really, especially when kicking heroin. A few turkey vultures circled overhead; Marlowe shook his head at the cliché.

On the way back, Marlowe debated whether to tell Chavez where Nestor was laid up. He remembered a law that stated wanted criminals could not be dragged out of rehab, and decided to keep mum. He felt grateful it wasn't' him kicking, twisting and turning, sleep impossible, unimaginable depression, every movement agony. The Beach Boys came on the radio again, and Marlowe felt a stab in the heart with every soaring harmony.

You know it seems the more we talk about it
It only makes it worse to live without it
But let's talk about it . . . Oh, wouldn't it be nice?

CHAPTER 35

D on Luis sat at a chipped formica booth at Grande Tortilla Factory, sipping his weak Nescafé. Juanita was outside in the Suburban and gave a little honk. He watched the Goat Lady enter, wearing an apron over a traditional huipil. She ordered two dozen large flour tortillas before sitting down at his table. How she knew it was him, he couldn't fathom—did he stick out that much? Before setting up the meeting, Juanita told him no one knew her real name, only that she came from an old Yaqui family that the growers of Guerrero and Michoacán trusted for generations to smuggle contraband.

Her face was like cracked plaster, with a few gold teeth here and there. Don Luis smiled at her gently and asked if she would like a champurrado? She replied that hot chocolate was a winter beverage, and it was only fall. He asked if she knew where her *sobrino nieto* was, and she told him Paco was living in an old Winnebago, set up behind a duplex she owned in a neighborhood called El Hoyo. Sotto voce, she pleaded with him not to kill Paco, said he was a good man living *una vida honorable.* Don Luis listened politely, not promising anything, but the phrase danced around his head like a ballerina.

Leaving Barrio Hollywood for El Hoyo, Juanita parked on 11th Ave by the Water Department. Don Luis entered the property through a white chain-link gate in the driveway. He ignored two chihuahuas raising hell in the front yard, and nodded at a gay couple lounging together in a plastic children's pool behind the rear unit. Opening another little wooden gate, Don Luis was charmed by a neat yard shaded by a well-pruned mesquite tree. A small ramada, with a ceiling fashioned from ocotillo, was bolted to the '70s-era RV. A wrought-iron table with three chairs sat on the adobe brick patio, while a rabbit-eared television blared a Mexican station. On the table were a few empty cans of beer and a dirty plate, attracting flies. Don Luis knocked softly, but no one answered.

He turned the knob slowly and opened the door.

"Paco? *Estás aquí?*"

Don Luis stepped up and into the Winnebago, revealing a clean and well-organized kitchenette, with a small sink and a fridge, and some bench seating with denim cushions. Homemade curtains, fashioned out of serape table runners, kept the sun out as an AC unit purred overhead. In the back was a bed, still freshly made, with a Mexican blanket on top. Don Luis was just ready to leave, when he got an urge to pee. A door halfway to the bed opened to a hard-plumbed porcelain toilet and a small shower with a Virgin of Guadalupe shower curtain. Don Luis lifted the lid and sighed in relief, thinking he could easily live in this hideout. He shook off and opened the shower curtain just out of curiosity. Paco was slumped in the corner, a bullet hole in his forehead, with another through his cheek. Don Luis swore under his breath and noticed a small silver crucifix hanging from Paco's neck. He yanked the cross off and pocketed it, murmuring a prayer as he zipped up. Calmly closing the RV's door behind him, he made his way back through the yard and to the street. The couple were still in the tiny pool, shades on and soaking up the rays. A voice called out to him.

"Hey, was last night a Mexican holiday or something? We heard firecrackers going off—scared our cat."

Don Luis pretended not to hear and averted their eyes. As he hopped back in the Suburban, Juanita asked him how it went.

"Hay más tiempo que vida—vamanos."

"Where to?"

"*La misión.*"

As Juanita drove west on 22nd, Don Luis thought about Paco meeting his fate in this profanity of strip malls and Circle K's. It was all so incongruous with the natural setting, a beautiful valley surrounded by mountains, now desecrated. His own pueblo, Cuernavaca, was a city of gardens and arroyos, created with at least some respect for the natural environment. He mused on Jenkins and his remote subdivision, out way beyond the amenities of central Tucson. Passing one empty lot after another, he couldn't imagine why this was allowed. What were they hiding from?

As they headed south, the desert slowly returned. A corner store advertised discount cigarettes, marking the beginning of tribal land. Don Luis sighed as he watched the familiar poverty of his own rural Mexico return. Casitas and trailers dotted here and there, yards full of broken-down cars and various metal objects, still too valuable to be considered junk. A few children were running around in the dirt, while their mother hung wet clothes from a line. An old man burning garbage looked up and stared, his face set in stone. As they passed a fenced dirt cemetery, a few marigolds still decorating graves, Don Luis could see the mission like a mirage in the distance. It reminded him of the churches the Dominicans built in La Mixteca, each a day or two horse ride apart, fortresses of faith and control. Juanita parked in the empty dirt lot, in front of *la paloma blanca del desierto*. Don Luis got out and told Juanita to keep watch.

Fingering Paco's crucifix, Don Luis approached the massive mesquite doors framed by bas-relief Christian imagery, along with native deities disguised to fool the Franciscans. He walked along a cactus garden rivaling any in Oaxaca, sublime in its selection of specimens and spacing. A thirty-something padre appeared in brown robes, coming out of his rectory with a young mother and son. Don Luis stood back while they said their goodbyes. The padre turned to go back inside, but paused when he saw the stranger.

"Buenos días, Padre."

"Good afternoon. I'm sorry, but my Spanish is lacking—a sin really."

Don Luis walked up and handed the crucifix to the padre.

"His name was Paco. Pray for him, *por favor, padre.*"

The padre looked down at the crucifix, then up at Don Luis.

"Were you related to him? *Era su amigo?*"

"No, padre, but he live *una vida honorable.*"

"I see, I see, but how did you get this if you didn't know him?"

Don Luis turned his back on the priest and strode back to the Suburban. As they drove off, Juanita remarked that a white van had circled the lot and left—some lost repair guy, she imagined. Don Luis sighed and wished it were so, but he knew better.

The hunt was on.

CHAPTER 36

The call came in just before 9 a.m., a request for a welfare check from an unidentified female relative. The patrol unit found a deceased male in the shower of a RV, with bullet holes to the head. On the short drive over from headquarters, Chavez hoped it was a suicide; he had enough going on. Arriving before forensics, he ignored some yapping dogs and a concerned neighbor and made his way to a Winnebago set up in the rear. The uniformed patrol explained how they found the body, while a TV blared a Spanish telenovela on the patio. Chavez put his coffee down next to some empty beer cans, then entered the RV to have a look. As soon as he saw the serape curtains and the Mexican blanket on the bed, Chavez knew it would be Paco.

"Well, you found the American dream, didn't you?"

Paco's eyes stared into the void.

"I should have made you go home to Hermosillo. I'm sorry, amigo."

Observing the position of the body, Chavez figured he'd been shot right here and slumped down. Not a lot of blood, probably a small caliber weapon. Seizing on the TV and beer cans, Chavez surmised they were probably watching soccer or a fight before Paco was marched back to the shower and killed. Using a pocket-pen–sized flashlight, Chavez examined all he could without touching anything. He noticed a very narrow band of lighter colored skin around Paco's neck, probably from a necklace. Yes, he remembered it now, a silver crucifix that Paco let hang outside his shirt. Bad time to lose it.

Grabbing his now cold coffee, Chavez went to talk to the neighbors who were gathered around an empty kiddie pool. An obviously gay couple, and middle-aged Latina lived in the two separate units. They seemed uneasy with one another, or maybe it was just his imagination.

"He's dead, isn't he?"

Chavez gave the couple a look that said yes.

"We knew this would happen. That Winnebago is not legal—the zoning doesn't allow for it."

The front neighbor piped up.

"Oh, be quiet, Justin, that RV's been here longer than any of you have."

Chavez asked about the landlord. They said they paid Paco in cash, who passed it along to his aunt. They had never met her, but Paco took care of all the yard work and maintenance.

"Did he have many visitors?"

"No, he was very quiet, right, Ines? We did see a man yesterday, around noon, we were in the pool. We heard him knock and call Paco's name, but he left soon after."

"What did he look like?"

"In his forties, I guess. Polo shirt, jeans, sunglasses. He looked like anybody."

"You see his car?"

"Ricky got the mail when he was back there, said there was a white Suburban out front with a young woman driving, right, Ricky?"

"Señora?"

"No, I was at work . . . I'm always at work, dealing blackjack at the casino."

"What about the night before?"

"We heard his TV, but that was normal. He watches outside for some reason—must be a Mexican thing."

Ines rolled her eyes.

"We did hear what we thought were firecrackers around eleven—scared Miss Judy."

"Miss Judy?"

"Our cat, she ran under the clawfoot tub, wouldn't come out til morning."

"Okay, the patrol guys will get your details. Thank you for your time."

"Was he murdered?"

"You'll learn it soon enough from the papers—yes, he was shot."

"Oh, my—a killer on the loose? Are we in danger?"

Ines rolled her eyes again.

"No, I highly doubt that, but here's my card. If you see anyone else snooping around, give me a call. I also wouldn't talk to the press if you want to maintain your privacy."

After waiting to consult with forensics, Chavez lumbered back to his car to go get some lunch. As he closed the driveway gate, Ines called out to him from her front yard, busy cleaning up dog shit.

"Detective, excuse me, but I didn't want to say anything in front of those two gossips."

"I understand—yes, señora?"

"He had a friend, slim Latino, muy guapo, drove a pickup."

"You saw them together?"

"Yes, a few times. They would leave in Paco's car."

"An Oldsmobile? Gold colored?"

"Yes, that's the one."

"What about the night before last—what time did you get home from work?"

"Around ten-thirty."

"Was the pickup out front when you got home from work?"

"No, only Paco's car, but it was gone in the morning, I figured he was at work. He had a city job, at a golf course I think."

"Anything else?"

"No, that's it. He was a nice man, fixed all sorts of stuff for me. I'd bring him some *cocido* when I made it—I think he really missed his family back home."

Chavez sighed, then got angry at himself for getting Paco killed.

"Yes, I'm sure he did—only four hours away, too, but might as well be the other side of the moon."

They looked at each other in mutual understanding. Chavez felt famished and thought about where to go for *caldo de res*, or *cocido* as she called it. He said goodbye and walked to his car, looking up and down the street for Paco's Oldsmobile, but it wasn't to be found. He felt her voice behind him like a breeze.

"*Que te vaya bien*, Detective. May God bless you."

CHAPTER 37

arlowe checked the mailbox, but only found bills and a flyer for life insurance. He'd decided to ignore Nestor's advice, and go home to wait it out. He didn't know exactly what was going on, but knew that hiding would only prolong the situation. His voicemail was empty as well—no message from La Española. Nada. Scared and angry, heartsick beyond repair, he sat down to write another letter.

Mi Querida,

I'm sure by now you have received my latest missive, but I have yet to hear a peep out of you. You must enjoy my torture, like a cat playing with a mouse before biting its head off. I suppose you are going out every night, teasing your pursuers, who want you even more since you are married. Yes, married in a church, do you remember? If you want a divorce, why don't you say so? Do you expect me, as always, to do all the work? Maybe you are still weighing your options, the promise of a green card worth a few more years with a junkie loser. Or perhaps, since my career is waning, there is nothing more to exploit for a groupie like yourself. Sometimes I think you are a cypher, a zero, devoid of any feelings, autistic. If you could only close your legs for a minute, or get off your knees in front of the latest sensation, perhaps you could find a minute or two to let me know JUST WHAT THE FUCK IS GOING ON?

Your husband,

Marlowe

Leaving the letter on the kitchen table, Marlowe fixed himself a sandwich and took it to the living room to catch the news. Murder in Barrio Viejo was the top story, a Mexican national shot. Marlowe watched as he ate, not really paying attention until a police official said they were looking for the victim's car, a champagne-colored Oldsmobile Cutlass Supreme.

No fucking way.

Feeling ill, Marlowe knew it was Paco. Who else could it be? He started to shake, feeling a cold chill as if he'd fallen through ice into a cold dark lake. He thought about calling Chavez, but what would that change? He was in deep shit, through no fault of his own—his reward for going straight. He wondered if he had enough money left to fly to Amsterdam or New York, any city with an active street drug market. One last run, overdose and be done with it. Why did he come back to Tucson anyway? What did he think he'd find? Salvation?

He took a long, hot shower, his breathing returned to normal, but he felt like he was outside his body, observing himself through a two-way mirror. He crawled into bed, tried to turn his mind off, but it was impossible. He had visions of George, Jenkins, Nestor, Roy, Chavez, their faces going in and out of focus, like a cheap noir movie.

Jesus fucking Christ!

Giving up on sleep, Marlowe went to the kitchen to make some chamomile tea. He thought about Nestor—whatever discomfort he was experiencing paled in comparison to the agony Nestor was going through. It was something to be grateful for. Seeing the letter, he sat down to read it again while sipping his tea. What was she doing at this very moment? Probably just getting home after another night out. Blood pressure rising, Marlowe added an even more vitriolic postscript, then got up to find an envelope and a stamp. Folding the letter carefully before sliding it inside the envelope, he licked and affixed the stamp, then wrote the address for the apartment they had shared in Madrid.

Fucking bitch.

Tea cold, he sat staring at the letter for a few minutes. Suddenly without thinking, hypnotized by some force, he walked through the dark living room and opened the sliding glass doors to the small patio outside. In a nearby palo verde, a screech owl hooted. Again, he felt like he was watching himself, disembodied from his physical self, a puppet on a string. He lifted the lid to a Weber grill, and grabbed a long BBQ lighter next to some tongs. He looked up at the stars, brilliant in the moonless night, and recognized Venus to the east. He lit the letter on fire, it burned a slow blue and orange as he adjusted his grasp, the envelope shrinking smaller and smaller before the last ember floated away into the night. The owl hooted again, followed by the barking of a dog, gently shushed by its owner.

Marlowe returned to bed, and immediately fell into a deep and restorative slumber. When he woke it was eight hours later, his first solid night of sleep since kicking heroin. Downing a double espresso, then taking a glorious shit, he felt like anything was possible. He got on the bike and soon found himself riding through the old neighborhood and down to the mesquite bosque again, the border between his past and the future.

CHAPTER 38

Arriving at the guardhouse at Tucson Country Club, Juanita gave her name and who they were visiting, then waited for the rent-a-cop to make the call before being waved on through. It really was a country of borders, Don Luis thought, the idea that it was a classless society a myth. Racism was the dominant force that defined the gringos, but classism came in a close second. Mexico wasn't much different, but it didn't pretend otherwise, and didn't lecture the rest of the world.

Impressed by the understated beauty of the homes, Don Luis could imagine living here, still in reasonable proximity to the rest of town. He noticed lawn jockeys in several yards, along with garden statues of sleepy Mexicans. Bunch of racist gringo assholes. Yet here he was, a poor street kid from Morelos, going to a meeting with the biggest son-of-a-bitch in town—and at *his* request.

They parked in the empty circular drive, and Don Luis instructed Juanita to stay put. Jenkins had assured him he would be alone, and sure enough the old man answered the door. They went back to his den, but wary of bugs, Don Luis remarked it was a beautiful day and perhaps they could talk outside? They sat down by the putting green, and Don Luis looked for signs of a wire on the old gringo, who noticed and shook his head. He unbuttoned his shirt, revealing a skeleton's chest.

"I understand your concern, but you have nothing to worry about. *No tienes nada de qué preocuparte.*"

"*Lo siento*, no be too careful, as you say."

"I received the bank transfer overseas, *recibí el dinero.* Tell your boss I'm very grateful, *estoy agradecido.* Do you understand?"

"Yes."

"I thought about what you said, *tu consejo*, that revenge is dangerous."

"Yes."

"*Quiero paz*, I want peace, *sin problemas con Sinaloa*."

"Yes."

"But we have another problem now."

"*Otro problema?*"

"*Hay un policia*, he's too close to our business, *husmeando*, sniffing around. I don't trust him, *no confío en él*."

"*Cuánta plata?*"

"He won't take money, *no quiere dinero*."

Don Luis knew where this was going. In a mesquite high above, a nosy thrasher was sounding the alarm, while a rabbit nervously traversed the putting green.

"He needs to disappear, *entiendes?*"

"*Esto es difícil, es mejor pagarle*, better to pay."

"He can't be bought off, *quiere destruirme*, to destroy me *pieza por pieza*."

"Name?"

"Chavez, Detective Chavez. He's the one *investigando* George's murder."

"Why kill a cop? *La venganza solo hice más problemas*."

Jenkins sighed and watched a twosome hit their approaches to a front pin; both came up short and would have difficult saves.

"He knows I killed someone long ago, *que tengo sangre en mis manos*."

"*Tiene alguna prueba?*"

"Proof? Does it matter? I trusted him, *confiaba en él*—that was a mistake. He wants to look into other things now, our business, *nuestros negocios—do you understand?*"

Don Luis nodded but stayed quiet, thinking. This *viejo* was becoming a problem. First he wants revenge, to pour gasoline on a fire, although he doesn't even know how his *pinche* grandson died. Now he wants to kill a cop he trusted, like a fool. Maybe it was better to just kill the old man? Call Polanco to get the okay? No, not after ten million just got wired to be washed through Rancho Maravilloso.

"*Voy a pensar en esto*, I need to think about this."

Jenkins spoke harshly, spittle flying from his cracked lips.

"Chavez has to die, *insultó mi honor!*"

"I understand, but *tengo que platicar con el jefe*, talk to the boss."

"If you won't do it, Sinaloa will—tell him that!"

Don Luis pretended not to hear, but was growing angry. He debated whether to spill the beans, how it would affect the outcome. This farce was nearly over, but could still turn out badly, endangering his own future.

"*La muerte de su nieto, fue un accidente.*"

"George? *Un accidente?* Impossible!"

"He fell, *se cayó de un carrito de golf, estaba borracho.*"

In shock, the old man translated for himself and the universe.

"Drunk? Fell from a *golf cart?* Who told you this? I don't believe it, *no lo creo.*"

"I am sorry, Señor Jenkins. *La muerte es cruel, y a veces absurda.*"

The old man froze, too stunned to ask for more details. Don Luis stood up, signaling the meeting was over. He had treated Tucson's patriarch with dignity and respect, but now the power balance had changed in his favor. There still was this cop to worry about, and Paco's murder was of concern, but his main task of maintaining the status quo was nearly complete. With a little luck, he'd be out of shithole Tucson and back in Mexico City in a few days.

They walked out front to the Suburban, Jenkins using a golf club as a cane. Don Luis wondered where he'd be at his age, hopefully in a nice compound back in Cuernavaca, with a pool and tennis court, all his trespasses forgiven. It was a lot to ask for, and he felt guilty for even thinking such a thing. Better to stay in the here and now and feel grateful for what you have. He'd come a long way, but it was a short fall down. Saying goodbye, they both looked up at a bicyclist riding past. Jenkins raised his club to point, then got a confused look on his face.

"No, no, it couldn't be."

"Señor Jenkins?"

The old man kept staring down the street.

"Nothing, my mind playing tricks. Remember what I said about the detective—he'll take us all down."

On the way out, the same guard signaled for them to stop so he could check the Suburban off his list. Don Luis handed a hundred to Juanita, who gave it to the guard with a condition.

"Just erase it, we were never here."

Making a show of it, the guard turned his pencil upside down and rubbed out the entry, then gave them a mock salute. Juanita returned the gesture then hit the gas.

"Where to, jefe?"

"I want to eat a club sandwich."

"You got it, boss."

As they passed an obscene life-sized dinosaur in front of a McDonald's, Don Luis smiled at the irony. The world was changing, and soon gringos like Jenkins would be equally extinct. In front of them, an ancient Honda Civic sported a *Keep It Simple Stupid* bumper sticker. Exactly, Don Luis thought, sound advice indeed.

CHAPTER 39

Chavez knew he shouldn't be playing golf, but when Marlowe called he couldn't resist. Marlowe was still involved after all—not quite a suspect, but more than a witness. Meeting at Fred Enke, they almost had the course to themselves, the snowbirds not in town for another month or so.

On the 8th hole, a relatively easy par-4, they took a moment to admire the majestic Catalinas from the elevated tee. A swarm of bees flew directly overhead, protecting the queen while searching for a suitable home. Reluctantly, Marlowe brought up what was on both their minds.

"It was Paco, right?"

"Yes. Should've never left Mexico."

"I went by Jenkins' house this morning on my bike."

Chavez looked at him funny.

"And why would you do that?"

"I don't know, I went for a ride and wound up down there."

"Did he see you?"

"I don't think so, but he was out front with this dude."

Chavez decided on a 3-wood and grabbed it from his bag.

"Okay, what did this *dude* look like?"

"Polo shirt and jeans. sunglasses, could have been anybody."

Chavez backed off the shot, and looked at Marlowe again.

"What was he driving?"

"A white Suburban, had a female driver. I got the license plate number."

Chavez felt high and nearly drove the green, then three-putted for bogey. Using his cell phone at the turn, he called in the plate number. It was registered to one Maria Juana Valdez with a Rio Rico address, no priors. He considered blowing off the back nine, but was only 2-over par, a sin not to finish the round. He tried to stay calm, but knew the case was cracking wide open, like a watermelon dropped from the moon.

On the 10th green, Chavez decided Marlowe deserved to know.

"He fell out of a cart drunk."

"Who did?"

"George Jenkins. They were out here fucking around, partying."

"Partying?"

"Celebrating a deal. Nestor had hooked George up with a new connection from Sinaloa, a few keys of meth every month. Paco was to drive it up from Nogales, and Jenkins' boy Roy had the biker distribution connections up into the Midwest. They met here after Paco got off work. A bottle came out, and they drove around the course like teenagers. Nestor took a turn too fast and George spilled out, hitting his head on the cart path. They rolled him into the trap and Paco raked it clean, then puked up the tequila he drank. Nestor told Paco to sleep it off in his car and call him as soon as George was found. He was worried about old man Jenkins and Sinaloa, too."

Marlowe lagged his putt a few feet shy and marked it, careful to be out of Chavez's line.

"Poor Paco. Who killed him?"

Chavez drained his ten-footer.

"I'm workin' on that, but Nestor dragged him into this shit."

"He's good at that—just look at me."

"You should have called it in when you found George—you did this to yourself."

Marlowe stroked his uphill putt firmly, the ball hitting the back of the cup, popping up in the air before plopping in the hole with a satisfying sound. He retrieved it while Chavez grabbed the flag.

"What *don't* we do to ourselves, Detective? Everything that happens is a consequence of prior actions or inactions. Yeah, I walked away from George, fuck him and his *abuelo*. I'm just trying to start a new life, you know? Clean up and maybe have a family one day with the woman I love. Is that so fucking wrong?"

Chavez saw the tears and knew better than to say anything more. He liked Marlowe—gringo was a decent golfer, took his medicine and never whined. Maybe not quite a man, but not a boy either, something in between.

They played the rest of the round in silence, then shook hands on 18 before walking to their cars. Thinking about what Marlowe said, Chavez decided to call Carmen again, maybe send some flowers her way. Life was too short to be too proud to beg, at least for the important things like love and forgiveness.

CHAPTER 40

Don Luis liked Gus Balon's place, filled with tradesmen and retired folk eating lunch. They had specials up on a board, similar to *comida corrida* places back home. He did get confused with how many different types of club sandwiches were on the menu—why complicate such a simple thing? Juanita recommended going with the traditional turkey breast, maybe with a cup of homemade soup. Don Luis was surprised how hungry he was, and how tasty the iced tea mixed with lemonade was. Before he left town, he wanted a big cowboy steak, maybe out at a place where they used to do business with the owner.

Juanita knew it well.

"Lil Abner's—there's money buried there."

Don Luis smiled.

"*Ah tesoro enterrado*—maybe some people, too."

Don Luis was surprised how fast his English was improving. If he lived here, he would be fluent in a year. He'd met expats in Cuernavaca who, after a decade, still couldn't speak proper Spanish. He never understood that kind of arrogance. He told Juanita to keep speaking English to him so he could practice.

"Jefe, remember that white van I saw at the mission? I think it's outside right now."

Don Luis took another bite and looked out the plate-glass window.

"You sure?"

"Yeah, see that twisted front bumper and cracked windshield? Exactly the same."

He took a look around the room, and noticed a scruffy looking white dude sitting by the cashier with a to-go order in front of him. He was dressed in painter's whites and black Converse high-tops, jailhouse tattoos on his arms. Definitely not a cop—probably Jenkins' muscle, Roy.

"*Sabes como matar*, you kill before?"

"No, jefe, never done any wetwork."

"*Dónde está tu pistola?*"

"Under the driver's seat."

"*Muy bien.* This sandwich have too much *mayonesa.*"

"*Has* too much—sorry about that, send it back."

"No, está bien. Next time I say?"

"Easy on the mayo."

"Easy on the mayo."

"Perfecto."

As they asked for their bill, Don Luis watched the man get up and go to the van. Back in the Suburban, Don Luis told Juanita to drive normal and head west to Saguaro National Monument. He'd seen pictures in a tourist brochure in his room and figured why not kill two birds with one stone?

"Gates Pass?"

"*Hay una vista bonita?*"

"Yes, jefe, beautiful view."

At a red light, Don Luis asked for the gun. Juanita reached under her seat and handed him the Glock. Don Luis did a press check to see if a round was chambered—yep, all good to go. Arriving at Gates Pass, they parked in the near empty lot. As they got out to climb the trail to the overlook, Don Luis watched the white van drive by, but knew it would be back. Sure enough, from above they saw it flipping a U-turn and headed back up the steep incline.

"Okay, Juanita, *regresa y espera*, go back and wait."

Don Luis noticed Juanita was shaking, which was good. It meant she was a human being, and knew this was no game. As she went back down the trail, Don Luis bushwhacked along a high ridge and circled back, just like he'd seen in a million Westerns as a kid. Sneaking a look, his luck held. The van was parked at the back of the lot, with a little arroyo behind. Don Luis scrambled down to the wash and climbed the bank, careful to stay hunched and out of the van's rear view mirrors. He slowly made his way to the open passenger-side window, then popped up like a prairie dog. The driver was staring at Juanita walking down the trail. On the seat next to him, a small caliber gun.

Don Luis raised the Glock.

"Roy?"

Startled, Roy reached for his gun, but stopped when he saw the barrel pointing at his head.

"Listen, I'm sorry, just following Jenkins' orders to keep an eye on you."

"I understand, this is for Paco."

Don Luis put a bullet in Roy's forehead, then calmly walked to the Suburban, where Juanita was hyperventilating behind the wheel.

"*Calmate, Juanita. Todo está bien.*"

"Where to, boss?"

"*El museo del desierto*, the Desert Museum, no?"

"*Está seguro?*"

"*Por qué no?* I want to see it, only live once."

Wiping the gun down with his handkerchief, Don Luis admired the terrain as they drove further west. Magnificent saguaros presided over the rocky desert, green and fat from summer monsoons. Surely this was one of the most special places on earth. Feeling a prickly pain, he looked down and noticed a spiked ball of cholla stuck to his trousers. He reached for his comb and removed it carefully, drawing a little blood.

Recognizing the word *picnic* on a sign, Don Luis instructed Juanita to turn into the area so they could dispose of the weapon. Finding a pull-out with a few vacant tables, Don Luis got out and looked for a good spot to dig. He swore at the hard caliche dirt, nearly gave up, then noticed a large hole high up in a three-armed saguaro. He made sure the safety was on and tossed the Glock up, but it bounced off, nearly hitting him in the head. Sweating profusely, he went back to the Suburban and asked Juanita to give him a hand. She stood up on a picnic table, and climbed aboard his shoulders like she was playing with her brothers at the beach. Don Luis staggered with her over to the saguaro, and on her first try the gun disappeared into the wood-pecker's lair. Elated, Don Luis let out a shout.

"Goooooooooool!"

At the Desert Museum, Don Luis took his time and studied each exhibit carefully. Juanita followed behind, looking pale, having crossed a moral divide never to return. Don Luis admired how they tried to pretend it wasn't a zoo, like a prison in Sweden or something. Coming to the Mexican Gray Wolves, he couldn't help but feel sorry for the *cabrones*. He'd never done time, not even a night in jail, and wondered if he'd be able to withstand it. He shuddered thinking about getting locked up here—at least in Mexico you could pay for decent treatment, hell, even run your business while eating home-cooked meals. Not liking where his mind was going, he told Juanita it was time to hit the gift shop, then back to the Arizona Inn. He bought a paperweight with a scorpion for himself, and a T-shirt with a silk-screened mountain lion for Juanita.

"Muchas gracias, Don Luis."

"Te mantuviste tranquila hoy."

"Kept my cool?"

"Yes, like a puma."

They drove back over Gates Pass. The parking lot was now a quarter full, but the white van was still parked alone in the back. With any luck, Roy would not be discovered until the lot closed after sunset. Back in his room, Don Luis took a long shower, scrubbing off the killing. Remembering Paco in the RV, he made a note to talk to the Goat Lady before he left, set things right. He would tell Polanco not to do any more business with Jenkins, and after the ten million was washed, eliminate him unless he croaked from natural causes first. As for the cop, he could sniff around all he wanted; good luck untangling this mess. The only loose end that nagged was this *cabrón* Marlowe Billings who stabbed Nestor—he just didn't fit into the frame. Why would a friend do that? And what were the chances he would be the one to discover George's body? Didn't Nestor say he'd been living in Madrid? Polanco moved a lot of coke through Spain, the main conduit to Northern Europe and the UK. Anything was possible. Maybe Sinaloa brought him in to set up a new pipeline—crazier shit had happened. Where the hell was Nestor anyway? Maybe he should order him to kill his buddy, revenge for that screwdriver in his guts, prove he's still a team player, as the gringos say.

Lying in bed, Don Luis thought of his mother and family back home. He would need to go to confession when he got back, maybe donate a few grand to that new youth center. Drifting off, he heard laughter from a nearby *casita* and the metallic squeal of a train in the distance.

CHAPTER 41

Chavez dreamed of Carmen. They were walking along a beach in Kino Bay, Tiburón Island, just offshore. Holding hands, they stopped to examine a bluebottle jellyfish, beautiful but dangerous. Chavez poked it with a stick, but the bubble wouldn't burst. A Seri Indian walked toward them, blankets and ironwood carvings for sale. Chavez reached for his wallet, but he was nude, as was Carmen. They laughed and laughed and ran into the surf—then a ringing in his ears.

"I'm sorry, Detective. I know it's early, but we have what appears to be a shooting at Gates Pass."

Groaning, back sore from his round with Marlowe, Chavez got dressed, swilled down some coffee, and drove in a daze to the crime scene. Just after 7 a.m., two patrol units were there with a park ranger, yellow tape already up. When he saw the white van, he knew it was Roy, Jenkins' goon. Instantly he was wide awake, adrenaline pumping, totally focused.

The body was slumped against the driver's side door, a bullet hole in his forehead, no exit wound. A 9-millimeter pistol was sitting on the passenger seat. Chavez spoke to the park ranger, a chunky middle-aged woman with a kind, sun-lined face.

"When did you call this in?"

"About an hour ago—6 a.m., I guess. I'm probably gonna get fired, but I noticed the van last night at closing. People like to sneak beer and wine up here to watch the sunset—they pass out in their cars all the time. I usually let them sleep it off and they're gone by morning."

"Asleep with a bullet in his head?"

"I only gave the van a cursory look driving by—like I said, it happens all the time. I'm gonna lose my pension over this, I just know it."

Chavez opened the glovebox with his *pañuelo* and carefully took out the registration: Leroy James Reynolds, 3274 E. Lonesome Trail. Well, you've rode your last round-up, Chavez thought—*vaya con dios*. Using the same handkerchief to pick up the gun, Chavez sniffed but could only smell gun oil; it had not been fired since cleaning. Thinking of Paco in the shower, his gut told him Roy's gun was the weapon that killed him. He put it back down for the forensics team, who'd arrived to take photos and dust for prints.

He looked around on the pavement, found a shell casing, and told one of the patrol guys to put an orange cone next to it. Backing away from the scene, Chavez motioned for the park ranger to join him.

"Did you tell anyone else about seeing the van last night?"

"No, just you."

"You didn't see it last night."

"Say again?"

"You didn't see it. You did your rounds but didn't see it."

"My supervisors won't believe me. How could I miss it?"

Chavez sighed. He looked up the hill as the sun lit up the pass. His eye slid along the ridge line, then down to an arroyo behind the van. A roadrunner walked by, curious about all the activity.

"Look, if you called in every drunk asleep in their car we'd be up here every night. You were keeping intoxicated drivers off the streets. How long have you been a ranger?"

"18 years."

"Okay, so don't throw it away. You never saw the van until this morning."

"I've always been honest in this job, never falsified a report."

"It has no bearing on my investigation, none. You have to decide now because I have my own report to write. So what's it gonna be?"

The ranger squinted hard at Chavez, eyes misting up.

"Thank you, Detective. I discovered the van this morning."

Walking back to the van, Chavez glanced up again at the pass, then behind to the arroyo. He could see it all happening in his head: Roy focused on the trail, while being bushwhacked from behind. Never saw it coming. More than he deserved after marching Paco back to his shower, making a mess of it with that first shot through the cheek.

Fucking amateur.

Driving to headquarters to type up the report, Chavez knew the Lieutenant would be waiting with the press breathing down his neck. It was time to call in the Suburban's plate, do an APB and felony stop, bring everyone in, including Jenkins and Nestor. There'd been enough killing, all because George Jenkins fell out of a stupid golf cart.

Stopping at St. Mary's Mexican Food, Chavez ordered a breakfast burrito loaded up with egg, potato, chorizo, cheese, and beans. Sitting by the front door reading the *Star* and waiting for his order, he felt a tap on his shoulder and looked up.

"Well, *hola, guapa*, I was just dreaming about you."

CHAPTER 42

Marlowe didn't quite know why, but he had to check on Nestor. His own habit was not nearly as severe, yet he still felt nasty symptoms of withdrawal on a daily basis. He dug around a backpack and found some leftover clonidine from rehab, and a grimy paperback of Rafael Bernal's *The Mongolian Conspiracy* to take him. Driving west into the sun, he thought about all the shit they did, the punk-rock life, and how drugs had taken their toll. He didn't owe Nestor anything, yet still felt this weird obligation. What did the literature say?

The therapeutic value of one addict helping another is without parallel.

He cruised past the turnoff, then found a place to flip a U-turn to see if anyone was following. Confident he was alone, he made his way down the dirt road and noticed the gate was open at the cattle guard. He drove through, then got out and closed it behind him, a few mildly interested steers watching from some shade. A few more miles in, he saw the crested saguaro, and found the parallel ruts that led to the shack.

Marlowe switched off the ignition and lightly honked the horn, hoping Nestor would come out happy to see him. Remembering the gun, he didn't want to think about what he might find. There was also the nasty business of the stab wound—sepsis can happen fast and kill within hours. He got out and approached the cabin, again feeling oddly detached, an actor in a play. He opened the door and everything looked the same, although the trash was full of empty soup cans and smashed flat jugs of water. The cot was made up like before, but the sleeping bag had some blood stains from the wound. On the table was the NA text, but no gun. He picked it up and noticed a torn piece of paper stuck inside.

Marlowe,

Caught a ride with some coyotes. If you're reading this it means you came back for me, so all is forgiven.

Nestor

Taking the book, Marlowe walked back to his car feeling relieved. Driving slow, he thought back to all his friends from the '70s. Some were in prison, others lawyers, teachers, what have you. Where he himself fit in, he didn't really know. One toe always in the gutter, he romanticized the outlaw life, but now realized he didn't have the stomach for it. Who was he fooling anyway? He was just another middle-class white boy, slumming through life, a bullshit artist supreme. It was time to if not grow up, then at least give up childish things, just like the thumpers say.

Approaching the cattle guard and gate, Marlowe tensed at the sight of a Border Patrol vehicle blocking the road.

Fuck.

He stayed in the car as the agent approached, an older white dude wearing aviator Ray-Bans and cowboy hat, just like Nicholson in *The Border*.

"License, please."

"Sure, but have I done something wrong?"

"Just routine, what are you doing out here?"

Marlowe fumbled with his wallet, and handed over his license.

"Just exploring—road wasn't marked as private."

"You weren't meeting someone out here, were ya?"

"Meeting someone? For what?"

"You tell me, maybe taking delivery of something. Mind if I look in your trunk? Let's both take a gander."

Getting out, Marlowe opened it up and they both peered in.

"Golfer, eh? I like to play some, but only par 3's. Great excuse to drink beer."

"I don't drink. I mean, I used to, but not anymore."

"Listen, you mind helping me out with something? I'll follow you back to that shack your buddy was holed up in, we can talk things over there."

Despite the heat, a cold shiver went down Marlowe's spine.

"Uh no, sorry. A friend is expecting me back in town. I have no idea what you're talkin' about."

"A friend? Who would that be?"

"Detective Chavez, Tucson Police Department."

"Son, I don't give a shit about no detective, we can do this the easy way or not . . . now who the fuck is that?"

Marlowe turned and saw the agent's cause of concern, a Chevy Silverado pickup pulling a horse trailer. The truck pulled up close, and an old cowboy got out dressed in classic Western garb that fit like a second skin. He approached them with an easy gait and grinned, but not too friendly-like at all.

"Well, well, if it ain't Frank Reynolds, slowest gun in the west."

"Afternoon, Carl. What brings you out this way?"

Marlowe noticed the agent's demeanor changed on a dime.

"Oh, same old shit—a vet's job is never easy. One of the Rex brothers' horses is in trouble, got the colic bad and needs surgery. Have to do it back in Tubac. Who've ya got there, a lost soul or something?"

"My name is Marlowe, Marlowe Billings—remember that!"

The cowboy cocked his head at Marlowe, then stared hard at the agent.

"Why sure, fella. I got me a good memory, never forget a face or name. Me and Frank go way back, don't we Frank?"

Deflated, the agent tried to regain control.

"Okay, Mr. Billings, you're free to go. Sorry for the inconvenience, but we have lots of smugglers out here, don't we, Carl?"

"Smugglers? *Contrabandistas*? Yeah, sure, along with dirty cops, right, Frank? Can't have one without the other."

Face red, the agent tried one more jab.

"How's your boy? Enjoying Florence?"

"Oh, he's just dandy, Frank—thanks for asking. What about your old partner, what was his name again? Randy Wilson? Happy to be in protective custody with the snitches and short eyes?"

The two old adversaries spat in the dirt and stared at each other, then went back to their vehicles. The agent backed up, letting Marlowe and the Silverado through. Marlowe returned to the main road, grateful his savior was right behind him. He thought of his folksy therapist back in rehab, and this old cowboy, cut from the same cloth. Maybe there *was* good to be found in this world, if only one stopped denying it existed. God?

Yeah, sure, call it whatever you want.

Back home, Marlowe jumped in the community pool, vacant as usual. He floated on his back, staring at the sky. A few clouds drifted past, but the rains were over till winter. Squirting water from his mouth like a whale, he watched a tarantula hawk wasp fly down to investigate. It hovered above his face, amber wings beating fast, could this be the same one? Marlowe dipped below the surface, musing that predators and prey were interchangeable. It was all one thing, a glorious mishmash of symbiotic survival. He realized he wanted very much to live, to see what happens next, enough of this death-tripping.

On the way home, he stopped to get the mail. Among the usual bills and flyers was a letter from Spain. He took it inside and felt the odd sensation of disembodiment strike again. He stripped off his trunks and wrapped himself in a towel, then sat down at the kitchen table. Using a paring knife, he opened the letter carefully and started to read.

Mi amor,

The other night, very late, I went out to the balcony to get some fresh air. I looked up at the sky, and saw what had to be a meteor, a shooting star. I realized life was no different, over before you know it, and what did I really want? If it's okay, I'd like to come to Tucson, and we can try again. It won't be easy, but life isn't either, and maybe we can turn all this pain and misery into something special.

Mil besos,

La Española

CHAPTER 43

They had one last powwow, sitting at a picnic table outside of Lil Abner's. Don Luis was amused at the size of his steak, enough for an entire family. The smell of mesquite smoke hovered in the air, and they all grew silent as the sun went down all orange and red. Don Luis helped himself to some beans and told Juanita what he wanted Nestor to hear.

"Don Luis doesn't like drug addicts. Normally he'd kill you. Tell him why he shouldn't."

Nestor pushed a beef rib around his plate, still in withdrawal; food was impossible.

"I've had my last run, jefe. Too old for this shit. If you want me to disappear I will."

Listening to Juanita translate, Don Luis looked at Nestor with contempt.

"*Como un cobarde*, like a coward?"

"I can lure Sinaloa in, wipe them out."

Don Luis waved a steak knife at Nestor.

"*Absolutamente no, Polanco no quiere más problemas.*"

Juanita took a big bite of rib and talked with her mouth half full.

"You get that?"

Nestor nodded, a beaten man.

"*Si mates a tu amigo, el anciano estuviera feliz.*"

"He says kill your friend, your buddy who stabbed you, old man Jenkins will be happy."

Nestor glanced at Juanita, then looked Don Luis in the eye and nodded.

"Está tan bien como hecho. You need a clean piece? I have one in my truck."

Juanita didn't bother to translate.

"Sure, go get it, I feel naked."

"Okay, gotta hit the toilet first, my guts are shredded, maybe change the dressing."

Juanita dropped her fork.

"Hey, we're eating here, *no seas tan crudo cabrón.*"

Nestor got up, took a quick piss inside, then went out to his pickup parked next to the Suburban. He removed his pistol from the glovebox, shoved it in his pants, then reached behind the bench seat and grabbed a tire-iron, duct tape, and a small package wrapped in black plastic. Squatting down, he pried a rear hubcap off the Suburban, taped the package securely inside, then replaced it with a few taps for good measure. Throwing the tire iron and duct tape into the bed of his truck, he returned to the table where Don Luis was practicing his English. The waitress came over to check on their table. Don Luis gave it a whirl.

"Dog bag, please."

"Doggie bag, boss."

"Doggie bag, please."

"Why sure, you like your steak okay?"

"Yes, ma'am, delicious."

"Glad to hear it, y'all want some pie with ice cream?"

"Pastel con helado, jefe?"

Don Luis looked at Juanita and Nestor, who both shook their heads.

"Just the bill, ma'am, and the doggie bag."

"Perfect, jefe. You'll be quoting Shakespeare in no time."

Business and meal over, they all got up and walked to the parking lot in the fading light. Nonchalantly, Nestor handed Juanita the pistol. A sorry-looking coyote, covered in mange, skulked by hoping for scraps. Don Luis threw it his half-eaten steak, then had one more bit of advice for Nestor as he got in the Suburban.

"The boss says if you get high again, take enough to overdose—because if he finds out, you'll be dead anyway."

Nestor snickered.

"Tell him not to worry. I might even retire and become a priest, save a few souls for the ones I've dispatched."

Juanita issued her own warning.

"Just make sure you kill your friend first. I'm in charge of Tucson now, he gave me a promotion."

Nestor laughed again.

"Congratulations, Juanita. Your uncle will be proud. Ain't this a great country? Home of the brave, land of the free."

CHAPTER 44

Chavez got the call at 9 a.m., an anonymous tip. He alerted the highway patrol, who pulled the Suburban over just south of Valencia on I-19, a female U.S. citizen and Mexican national inside. At his desk, just a few minutes away, it seemed like hours as he sped down to the location. He arrived at the same time as a K-9 unit, regular procedure with felony stops so near to the border. The suspects were still in the vehicle, and Chavez took a quick look at a driver's license and border crossing card before approaching the driver's side window.

"Good morning, folks. I'm Detective Chavez from Tucson Police Department—may I ask where you're heading?"

"Just giving my friend here a ride back to the border."

"He's a little far north, isn't he? Certainly beyond the 25-mile limit for a crossing card."

"Yeah, sorry 'bout that. He wanted to see his sister in Tucson."

"Say, you don't have any weapons in the car, do you?"

The driver looked at the passenger, who nodded his head ever so slightly.

"Actually I do, officer, a handgun under my seat."

"Is it loaded?"

"Yes, it is."

"Are you licensed?"

"No, I'm not."

"Anything else?"

"No, that's it."

"Okay, I'm gonna ask you both to get out and wait at the front of your vehicle. Keep your hands on the hood and refrain from conversation."

"May I ask what this is about, officer? Sorry about the gun, but you can't be too careful with all the carjackings going on."

"Oh, just routine, your vehicle matches a description of one we're looking for."

Chavez instructed the patrolman to keep the suspects company, then got out his handkerchief and carefully removed the pistol from under the seat. He sniffed the barrel and thought about where they stood: an unlicensed carry and a border violation. The gun smelled clean, and the wrong caliber to be involved in Roy's murder. As for the Mexican national, dude gave off very heavy vibes. Chavez looked back at the K-9 unit and motioned for them to do a drug check, but doubted it was worth the effort.

The K-9 handler was a young woman, and as she walked by with the leashed Belgian Shepherd she gave Chavez a playful wink. He thought of Carmen, and how intense it was to make love to her again. They'd spent the evening enjoying each other's company, no serious discussions, no recriminations, just sweetness. In the distance, San Xavier Mission seemed to radiate peace and tranquility. He felt happy about Carmen, but exhausted from the job. He thought back to his cousin Johnny and realized he could never bring him back, or La Calle, any of it. He was alive in the here and now—it was all he had, and he better not waste any more time.

"Detective . . . Detective?"

Chavez snapped out of his reverie and glanced up at the K-9 officer. She pointed to the dog, who was sitting next to the passenger side rear wheel, whining off and on. He looked at the suspects, the Mexican national was shaking his head, while the driver was frantically whispering to him in Spanish. On a hunch, he went to the Crown Vic's trunk, grabbed a tire iron, and pried off the Suburban's hubcap.

Bingo!

Sometimes it was just too easy . . .

EPILOGUE

The boy had no bad habits to start with—his swing was a blank canvas, his mind saw only what was possible. As soon as he could walk, Marlowe put a toy club in his hands, and he whacked plastic balls all over the townhouse. La Española poured her love into the boy like nothing else on earth—indeed for her, there *was* nothing else that mattered.

Marlowe didn't mind. He joined a house-painting crew of recovering addicts, then worked for a real-estate appraiser he met while playing golf. The job took them all over Southern Arizona, and they often had afternoons off to explore an undiscovered course, trying to get the last few holes in as the sun went down.

La Española went back to school, studying the poets she held dear: Machado, Darío, Wilde. The Modern Languages Department adored her, and she soon advanced to the Ph.D. program, becoming the intellectual she never thought possible. Marlowe was proud of her accomplishments, but was unable to express himself artistically, having already shot his wad as a young man. Regardless, he loved her and their child with all his being—surely that was enough to keep a man happy.

The boy got better and better. At the range, his natural shot was a high, soft draw. The only thing Marlowe insisted on was a proper grip; the rest he picked up by himself. Adults would watch the toddler hit, shaking their heads in wonder, surely a prodigy in the making. He spoke and understood English and Spanish equally, loved Thomas the Tank Engine, and his dear *abuela*, who often visited from Spain.

One day, reading the paper while watching the boy play, Marlowe learned that Jenkins had died after collapsing at home. The maid called 911 after finding him on the putting green, but nothing could be done. It was noted he'd been an avid golfer and was largely responsible for Tucson's growth and economic success after World War II. In the days that followed, tributes poured in, letters to the editor extolling Jenkins' efforts, and how grateful Tucson should be to have had such an exemplary city father.

Marlowe kept Nestor's note tucked into the NA text, but never heard from him again. He did hear rumors about a crime spree with the daughter of a rock star, the veracity of which it was impossible to know. Grum he saw rarely, their lives growing further and further apart. He still golfed occasionally with Chavez, who now had a daughter roughly the same age as the boy, and was working himself through law school after quitting the department. They rarely spoke of George's murder, if indeed it was murder, and not just a stupid accident like Paco claimed. Chavez did tell him Roy shot Paco, and that Roy was killed by cartel members who were now serving time in Florence on a minor trafficking beef. It all seemed like a faded dream, or a cheap crime novel one half-reads while lying sunburned on a beach.

Marlowe still liked to ride his bike down through Indian Ridge, and into Tucson Country Club. He was clean now going on a half decade, and exercise was great for releasing endorphins and keeping anxiety at bay. One day, passing Jenkins' house, he noticed a for-sale sign in the empty driveway. The putting green was still there, but overgrown with weeds. Reflexively, he touched his head and felt the sore spot on his skull, never fully healed. Chugging back up the hill, he felt liberated from the past, and wondered what he should cook his family for lunch. Putting the bike away, he saw the same tool bucket he'd grabbed the screwdriver from, and shuddered at the memory. Inside, La Española was sitting at the kitchen table, with a letter in her hand.

"It's from CUNY—they've offered me a tenure track position. What do you think, should we move to New York?"

Marlowe gulped like a fish yanked onto shore, the ground beneath swallowing him up. He was prepared for Boulder, or Charleston even, but New York City? He knew then and there his marriage was over, and felt the camera pull out wider and wider until he was only a speck. It would take another decade for his life to completely unravel, but that's another novel entirely.

ABOUT THE AUTHOR

Dan Stuart is an author & musician most noted for being the leader of 80's LA band Green on Red, and more recently his series of Marlowe Billings books and records.